Khadija Marouazi is a professor of literature at Ibn Tofaïl University in Kenitra, Morocco, and a human rights activist. She is a member of the scientific committee for the Moroccan magazine *Dafatir al-sijjin* (Prisoner's Notebooks), and the general secretary and founding member of the organization al-Wasit min Ajl al-Dimuqratiya (The Mediator for Democracy and Human Rights). *History of Ash* is her first novel.

Alexander E. Elinson is associate professor of Arabic and head of the Arabic program at Hunter College of the City University of New York. He is the translator of *A Beautiful White Cat Walks with Me* and *A Shimmering Red Fish Swims with Me* by Youssef Fadel, and *Hot Maroc* by Yassin Adnan.

T0007075

History of Ash

Khadija Marouazi

Translated from the Arabic by
Alexander E. Elinson

hoopoe
AN IMPRINT OF AUC PRESS

First published in 2023 by Hoopoe
113 Sharia Kasr el Aini, Cairo, Egypt
420 Lexington Avenue, Suite 1644, New York, NY 10170
www.hoopoefiction.com

Hoopoe is an imprint of The American University in Cairo Press
www.aucpress.com

ISBN 978 1 649 03281 2

Library of Congress Cataloging-in-Publication Data

Names: Marwāzī, Khadījah, author. | Elinson, Alexander E., translator.
Title: History of ash / Khadija Marouazi ; translated by Alexander E.
    Elinson.
Other titles: Sīrat al-ramād. English
Identifiers: LCCN 2023009696 | ISBN 9781649032812 (trade paperback) | ISBN
    9781649032829 (hardback) | ISBN 9781649032836 (epub) | ISBN
    9781649032843 (adobe pdf)
Subjects: LCGFT: Prison fiction. | Novels.
Classification: LCC PJ7846.A736 S5713 2023 | DDC
    892.7/37--dc23/eng/20230306

1 2 3 4 5   27 26 25 24 23

Designed by Adam el-Sehemy

Introduction
Alexander E. Elinson

KING HASSAN II (D. 1999) RULED MOROCCO with an iron fist from 1961 to 1999. Following two attempted coups, one in 1971 and another in 1972, and significant leftist pro-reform activity that sought to challenge the regime's autocratic rule, Moroccans suffered crackdowns on popular protest, limitations on freedom of expression and the press, sham trials, torture, mass arbitrary imprisonment, and forced disappearances. The Years of Lead of the 1970s and 1980s were a time of considerable brutality and fear in Morocco, and it was only in the 1990s that Morocco's human rights record began to improve as a result of both Moroccan and international human rights activities. With this improvement, starting in the early-2000s, Moroccans expressed themselves as never before in the form of published written material (prison memoirs, poetry collections, and novels), cinema, and public forums that included television airings of testimonials. As in Youssef Fadel's *A Rare Blue Bird Flies with Me* (published by Hoopoe) and other similar works, *History of Ash* by Khadija Marouazi is lyrical and powerful. It provides a close-up view of the physical and psychological hardships prisoners endure in prison and the damage that comes as a result, the challenges they face upon release, and the toll all this takes on families and friends alike. At the same time, the novel never gives up hope and speaks to the power of the written and spoken word to bring about solace and justice.

History of Ash is a fictional prison account narrated from the point of view of two characters, Mouline and Leila, both of whom have been imprisoned for their involvement in leftist/Marxist pro-democracy movements. The novel moves between the present and the past, providing personal and gendered narratives of experiences lived inside the prison cell, the torture chamber, the courtroom, and outside the prison walls. Through these main narrators, we also meet fellow comrades in the struggle to bring social, economic, and democratic reform to Morocco. Marouazi makes clear that striving for control of the narrative is an essential act, and that the sum of public expression detailing Morocco's dark past, and its documentation, is essential to the country's ongoing reconciliation process. Narratives such as these stand in the face of an official discourse that, until the 1990s, held a virtual monopoly on Moroccan history. Despite the government's embrace of the language, and even the spirit of human rights to some extent, it is still a realm that the government aims to control—when to talk about it, how to talk about it, and when the discussion is over. Creative works about the prison experience, on the other hand, provide voices and versions of events that seek to subvert official narratives in favor of histories told from many points of view that are much more inclusive of Moroccans' many experiences of the Years of Lead. These diverse voices pose a direct challenge to the regime's attempt to impose its singular reading on Moroccan history and reality. Memory and storytelling play key roles in the novel as the two narrators, Mouline and Leila, recall their experiences as activists, prisoners, and engaged citizens. These characters narrate the details of their imprisonment and of their goals of freedom (both personal and national) in stark detail. Like modern-day Shahrazads, their storytelling takes on an essential, life-saving quality without which the prisoners and their stories would fade into hopeless oblivion.

The novel weaves its way through lyrical, abstract, and stream of consciousness narratives that underline the often-confusing sense of the passage of prison time and memory. Also, it includes frank and concise reflections on freedom, captivity, betrayal, and human relationships in all their complicated messiness. There are references to Palestinian poets Samih al-Qasim (d. 2014), Mahmoud Darwish (d. 2008), Mu'in Bsisu (d. 1984), and Mourid Barghouti (d. 2021), whose politically engaged poetry is such an important part of the contemporary Arabic poetic canon, and whose work serves as touchstones and inspiration for people across the Arab world. Marouazi also opens up narrative dialogues with novelists such as Haidar Haidar (b. 1936) from Syria and Abdul Rahman Munif (d. 2004) from Saudi Arabia, both of whom wrote about autocracy, corruption, liberation movements, and prison. This literary engagement is not limited to the Arab world either, with nods to Greek author Niko Kazantzakis (d. 1957), Belgian poet and writer Henri Michaux (d. 1984), and the Spanish author of the classic *Don Quixote*, Miguel de Cervantes (d. 1616). This extra-textual meandering should come as no surprise as Marouazi is a scholar and professor of literature. But more than serving as mere references, through them, Marouazi reminds us that art and the creative spirit are universal and can serve as powerful means of resistance in a world filled with cruelty, ignorance, darkness, and ugliness. About one particularly vivid passage in which the narrator recalls the paintings of Armenian-Lebanese painter, Paul Guiragossian (d. 1993), Marouazi speaks of the extreme difficulty of describing torture, especially the torture of women. When language falls short, other means of expression and inspiration are necessary. In this particular passage, in striving for the appropriate language to describe the indescribable horror of the torture chamber, the author turns to the visual evocation of Guiragossian's violent strokes, vivid colors, and grotesquely beautiful stretched out bodies.

History of Ash is a work of literary fiction that aims to both document the prison experience and humanize it. It draws inspiration from the vast archives of testimonies, writings, and articulated experiences of former political prisoners (Moroccan and otherwise) and tells a brutal and tender story that ultimately provides hope and paves a way forward.

Part One

Good morning, Gharbia

1

THE SEA . . . THE SEA. I will only turn toward the sea. It is what my soul has held onto for these twenty years. I will not turn toward the prison gate. Whenever Mama would visit, she would insist, and when she no longer came, she would pass along this advice through Leila or other friends: "Mouline, don't turn toward the prison. That way you won't go back. That's all I ask. Don't turn toward the prison gate!"

Then she would add these words—which came to sound like the invocation of God's name as one year followed another—with a sense of suffering and expectation that continues to eat away at me: "Whether I'm alive or dead, don't turn toward the prison gate. Push forward, and don't look back. That way, you'll never return."

But what remains of life after twenty years spent in a cement chamber? Twenty years swallowed up by the cold walls and the echo of slamming prison doors. What life remains other than this trifle which will throw us directly from prison into the hospital, where we'll talk about it for the rest of our lives? After the walls have sown their long-lasting poisons in us so we can harvest those illnesses all at once, those illnesses that had been planted in us bit by bit. I will turn my gaze from the prison gate and face forward, toward the sea. Because Fate insisted on taking all of Mama's other wishes from her, I had no choice but to grant her this one request. I will not turn back, but how will I know which way the sea is?

3

When we entered Gharbia on that cold dark night, we entered its prison, not its civic space. We entered its prison cells, not its streets. We arrived in groups over the course of twenty-one days. We were brought in at night so we wouldn't be noticed. Would I know the way to the sea? Poetry can often act like a compass that keeps you from getting lost. This is where Salah once said,

> A prison
> A graveyard
> A sea
> from prison
> to prison, I will always flee . . .

Salah said it when the sea was far away. I took two more steps. The graveyard seemed to be spread out over a hillside, with us on the plateau, trapped there like the Prophet Jonah in the belly of the whale. But how did Salah know the geography of this place? Out of all of us, he was the one who had his face pressed up against the prison van's window when it took us to the hospital. Salah looked out the window, smiling like a child who had lost his toy and was determined to get it back. He looked out and smiled because his toy appeared before him, just a stone's throw away, just outside the window. It might have been because he remained there transfixed and saw a funeral procession carrying a corpse that he knew the graveyard was near the prison. As for the sea, no one could not know it was there. Even though its dizzying light continues to envelop me, it was a close friend through fall and winter, its waves crashing down, echoing and knocking on the cell doors. That's how all beautiful things are in my country . . . they only come as echoes and rust. I don't know how my connection to it began, but I am sure that even before I get out, I won't love it until it has expelled all the bodies it swallowed up over the summer. I offer myself to it in the fall, and commune with it in the winter. Twenty years in the central prison, and the sea stood by with all its strength, especially when the frost began to breathe its poison into our joints. It was an intimate friend; particularly at night when silence blanketed that desolate place; it would creep in, whispering. The sea is a woman when there is no woman at hand . . . but now, it is practically still. Scattered rain falls here and there. I raise my face up into it as if performing my ablutions.

When I was called in to see the prison warden, I was surprised by their decision to release me one week shy of completing my twenty-year sentence. Of course, Leila wouldn't be waiting for me. I knew that measures had been taken to keep the press and our comrades away, what with the feverish welcome they would bring along with them. However, their measures, no matter how skillfully devised, were as fragile as a pistachio nut. Families, friends, and members of the press would be lined up in front of the prison gate for weeks before the appointed time, waiting for the release of their loved ones. But Leila would come for her regular visit and wouldn't find me. Only she knows how much I love the sea. She would often follow me down the corridor asking,

"Me or the sea?"

"Both of you at the same time."

"Then I'll hang back for a bit and let the sea visit you."

I grab her wrists and lift them up a little, pressing them to my chest, hot with the thirst of many years. Leila doesn't know that I could not love the sea without her. Leila is always moist. Every time she visited, I would embrace her. I would kiss her hair which smelled of the sea.

I walked to the middle of the beach, a steady rain falling on my face. If Leila were here, the drops would look like a string of precious stones scattered across her marble-like neck. I leaned against a mound of sand I had formed with my hands. I moved them back and forth a little. The mound dissolved as soon as the water came up to the sand. I felt spent. I tried again but didn't get much further than I did the first time. I leaned over to pull a half-buried oyster out of the sand. Gently, I brushed it off and held it up to my nose. It smelled like Leila. Slowly, I did it again as if I were a drowning man rising up out of the water to fill his lungs with air. I studied the oyster carefully, wiping it off again, and put it to my ear. I pressed on it a little bit, then again, when suddenly, I was struck by a loud sound . . . something like scraping on wood. No! Rather, on leaves. I felt my body grow heavier. Slowly, I lowered myself. The blood ran hot to my ears. I let the sand grab me. The oyster's echo still rang in my ear and filled it, taking on the echo of those wasted years, there, where my body lay a great distance from me. I put my hand—my fingers—on my leg and couldn't tell whether or not they were mine. My thighs. My legs. My waist. Everything was dry and withered. It was the dryness that scared me. Every time I placed my hand on a part of my body, it was as if I were putting it on a piece of damp wood, until, after three days when the fog of the blindfold began to lift, I discovered that I was one of the walking dead. My body was becoming frighteningly emaciated. My discoveries came in fits and starts. I continued to break down under torture. I was dizzy all the time. As soon as I woke up and touched my body, I broke down again. Then I would disappear into a slumber and wake up to the sound of something scratching and scratching underneath my body which was stretched out on a bed of cardboard. The scratching continued, which got to me. The sound began to shoot from under this bed directly to my ear. Violently, and with considerable effort, I pulled my body up. I grabbed the cardboard and shook it a little hoping that the source of the scratching sound would fall from one of its folds. I got down on the floor to look into some of the holes there. In the right-hand corner, I discovered a burrow. I threw myself to the opposite corner. There was a tail curling up into it quick as a flash of lightning. I held my breath. The tail disappeared inside, and then the head appeared. It was a mouse! With what remained of my strength, I rushed to the door and started to bang on it. I was screaming at the top of my lungs when the Hadj (all the guards had us call them "hadj") came over to my cell. He took his keys out. I didn't know what he was expecting me do. I didn't know what I was expecting *myself* to do after all this screaming. I surprised him with a request to go to the toilet.

Up until when he inserted the key into my cell door's lock, I didn't think I was going to ask him for anything other than to get rid of the mouse and fill the hole with cement. I don't know what compelled me to ask to go to the toilet.

"All you people are good at is going to the toilet. If only you would exchange your shit for words, it would be better for you and us both, for God's sake!"

That's what the Hadj said as he flung open the door of my cell in my face. Had I revealed the truth of the matter, I would have handed them my point of weakness on a silver platter. It was a good distance from my cell to the toilet, and I had to walk between two facing rows of cells. The Hadj's stick rushed me along. I pushed the door open and went in. I opened my fly and peed with some difficulty as there was nothing there really. All I wanted was to stall for time so I wouldn't have to go back to the cell. Perhaps if I took my time, it would leave and go someplace else. The problem with the hole was that another one might appear at any time. *Ya Rabb*. Dear God! I've got to get a hold of myself. I'll try. I'll try. The Hadj knocked twice and yelled,

"Hurry up. Are you constipated?!"

I came out clearing my throat, my hand on my fly. I dragged my feet as the Hadj shoved me back into my cell. He locked the door and left while I stood on my tiptoes, back pressed up against the door. I fixed my gaze on the opposite corner, on the mouse hole where that little silvery-grey creature had forced me to play blind man's bluff again after all these years. The other kids used to insist that I join them, and when my turn came around and I covered my eyes, they would take the opportunity to grab onto anything small and limp—a knotted up piece of wool or even some clothing—and throw it at my face.

"Mouline, look out! A mouse, a mouse!" They would jump up and run away while I stood there, hopping up and down, terrified. I would scream at the top of my lungs. I would cry. And when I found the fake thing they had thrown at me, I'd chase after them, loading my hands up with rocks and filling the alley with screams. It wouldn't end until Youssef convinced me to fall for it again, whenever his turn came in the game of blind man's bluff.

Good God, the mouse was back after all this time. I'll play the game again here and now, even though this is no place for games. I got tired of standing. There was no trace of it. I moved the cardboard a little toward the door so I could sleep as far as I could from the mouse hole. However, I worried that this would make the Hadj suspicious, so I pushed it into the middle of the cell and lay down. I stretched out and relaxed a little but couldn't put the little silvery-grey mouse out of my mind. I began to reassure myself by comparing its size to mine. What could it do to me compared to what the agents do to my body? Could I take all of that and then give in to this silvery-grey mouse? No, no way. I tried closing my eyes. In vain, I tried to get as far away from it as I could.

Three days of fitful tossing and turning, waking up at the slightest sound—the jangling of keys, one of the comrades heading to the toilet, another one crying out in pain. I was wound up as tight as a clock, ready to jump at the slightest noise. The room became even gloomier. I kept my eyes open until they were puffy and bulging. Perhaps I would catch a glimpse of it. It was dark grey when I saw it during the day-time. Maybe it had left and another, or others, had come in its place. Who knows? I never knew before that there was something called "morning" in here. But the presence of this silvery-grey mouse forced me to make it out, or at least to imagine I had. It was only then, in the morning, that it was possible to see the hole, and to keep track of the mouse's comings and goings.

But how did I fall asleep one morning only to wake up with something scurrying over my outstretched hand, causing me to start screaming again as it went into its hole? The Hadj opened the door and came in with two agents who blindfolded me and dragged me to the "hospitality" session. I didn't ask for the toilet. I didn't even think about the torture rituals. We had been detained for more than two years between the secret prison and garde à vue. The judicial police would take us to the district attorney and the investigating judge. They would put their cigarettes out on us and use us as practice dummies for their whips. I learned from the prison doctor afterwards that, with us nine, he could not figure out why our wounds kept reappearing despite our transfer to this location more than three months prior. In contrast, the wounds and scars on the rest of our comrades had stopped bleeding and appeared to be healing more or less. I asked him about the names of the nine comrades, and he told me about four of them, referring to them by their numbers: 11, 33, 78, 104. After two years in the Derb Moulay Cherif secret prison, we had not met one another either as numbers or names. We were constantly separated and moved from prison to prison and kept from interacting with one another. All I knew was that number 11 was Salah Ribaoui. He was next to me for the first six months.

Whenever my number was called, I knew that he would come next. We got to know each other better when we crept toward one another at night, when the torturer's whip had let up a little. Blindfolded with hands and legs bound, one would lean up against the other one's back. When Salah asked me for the first time what my name was and learned that number 33 was Mouline Lyazidi, he let out a joyful yell and offered his number and name: "I'm Salah, number 11. Salah Ribaoui. We belong to the same organization." He informed me that the seven numbers with us in this room belonged to the Fatah al-'Ilmi organization. I didn't know Salah that well, but I had heard of him as a movement member who studied philosophy. However, only poetry could calm his heart. Once, I saw him reciting poetry at a demonstration at the university, but the heat of the moment had forced him to be quiet. No one could deal with poetry about love or twilight or birds. Everyone was feeling the heat of that day with its roaring slogans that roiled our blood, until the moment when poetry was born in the middle of all that fever-pitched excitement. Salah Ribaoui stepped down from the podium amid whistles and screams, dripping with sweat. The rising tide of people was listening only to itself, listening only to the clamor. When we met one another in the police station, we recounted the story and broke out laughing, Salah saying,

"Brother, had everyone in that crowd who believed in just causes understood the meaning of love—which they say doesn't matter—before embracing these larger issues, none of this would have happened."

"But then, as now, there was no connection to love. It was all about authority. What will change my love for a woman, or a poet, or a friend, or a comrade, while the government continues to oppress me, keeping us in custody all this time? Love. Love is what *they* need to know—the agents, the authorities. They're the ones who need to hear the call, not us," I replied.

"But we're also in need of such an education. Whenever I think about our petty differences and how they've become so central to the point where we draw our weapons against one another, I swear, I say to myself that it's love we're missing. We're missing love . . . and other things, of course."

When the doctor mentioned number 11 to me, I let out a laugh he didn't understand. Now you have all the time in the world to teach us the A-B-Cs of love, Salah. I swear, you can use all the current titles: *Love Between Hammer and Nail. Love Is Boundless Reality. How Did We Come to Love One Another in Just Six Days?*

I don't know why they continued to interrogate the nine of us. The torture session lasted for more than four hours. Even though it seemed that they only had one question, it took on multiple forms. They were trying to get to the bottom of the whole affair, from its origins to its purported goals. The interrogation at this particular point followed another path. Were we in favor of the country annexing the Kida region? That was the question that would later form the center of the case, at a time when the movement itself was not in agreement on it. Up until the time we were arrested, the matter had not been laid out officially or unofficially, despite the fact that preparations had already begun to incite both popular opinion and the nationalist parties against us on this very point. The annexation of this area was a sacred matter, and it was inevitable that the issue would cause chaos and delay because of a handful of disruptive groups. Thus, everyone sensed that another scenario was starting to come together—added to all of those other scenarios which had been broken up until now by our resistance in order to nourish campaigns to eradicate illiteracy and sweatshops, and to work in conjunction with cultural and educational groups. All of this was directed toward an awareness of how necessary it was *not* to include the Kida region as part of the country. Thus, charges of conspiracy and attempting to overthrow the regime would be cheapened and could be achieved only by the pen, as Lalla Aicha put it when her son Khalid was sentenced to ten years. She screamed at the presiding judge in the courtroom,

"Why? Why? My son is only sixteen years old!"

"Because he tried to overthrow the regime."

"Is there a regime that can brought down with pens? My son and all these nice young men . . . What have you seized from our houses other than pens, papers, books, newspapers, and magazines? You need gunpowder to overthrow a regime!"

Lalla Aicha screamed in the faces of the reinforced guard detail and security cordon in the courtroom until she fainted.

Khalid was the youngest prisoner among us. He was still in high school. The case was beset with confusion for some time, as the defense had made our trial an example of the kind of rights violations our case included. The defense insisted that Khalid alone be released, seeing as he was still a minor, even though the presiding judge viewed release as unlikely. The counsel argued for special consideration to transfer him to a juvenile rehabilitation center. This was before the surprise order came down stating that the presiding judge should deal with our cases as one, not separately. Khalid beat them to the punch, though, when he refused his transfer to a rehabilitation program, insisting on standing trial with his comrades. He stepped forward and yelled in front of the judge's bench,

"Wherever you take me, I won't choose any education other than the one that landed me here!" Khalid was short, and because he was so close to the judge's bench, the judge could not see him at all and had to lean forward in his seat in order to see the little fellow making all this racket.

Before he could finish what he was saying, Khalid was cut off by our chanted slogans, something we would do time and again whenever someone voiced their defiance. This of course, angered the public prosecutor, prompting him to request that the proceedings be postponed, which only resulted in more shouted slogans. The presiding judge tried to school us on slogan-yelling and clapping, telling us that this type of behavior was not allowed in the courtroom. One of the members of the defense team cut him off, saying,

"If we were truly in a normal courtroom, we could include our voices with that of the presiding judge. However, we're in a court which is itself a farce. How can we pass judgment on these young people for expressing an opinion? It's as if we're passing judgment on the fact that the year includes springtime, or that spring is filled with roses."

This point was enough to make us burst out again into songs and slogans, denouncing the violations against us, and praising the defense's abilities.

The judge appointed to head the proceedings had no prior experience with criminal cases. He had always worked in the civil sphere and people wondered why the criminal court had entrusted him with this task. But as soon as the proceedings began, once the presiding judge was sure that everyone was present and he refused to allow the court stenographer to read the referral, with the justification that it consisted of too many pages and would just waste time, everyone came to understand that this judge was appointed because of his ability to push things to the extreme.

While the question of my position on the inclusion of the Kida region in our nation was tracing bloody lines all over my body and placing electric shocks and cigarette burns on all my joints and my genitals, I remained obsessed with that mouse. Had it gone into its hole? Had it come out? For the first time, I was distracted from the torture by other things. My responses to their questions remained circumscribed.

"Is your secret organization in favor of Kida's annexation or not?"

"We're still organizing ourselves internally. Our discussions only deal with planning and general principles. This issue hasn't been introduced yet."

"Son of a bitch! And eradicating illiteracy? Meeting with workers? Posters and announcements? These are what you call 'organizing principles' and 'structural planning?!' Talk, you piece of shit, or I'll break you in half!"

They cut me off with a strong slap to the face. I felt a warm rivulet of blood flowing from my nose (I often got nosebleeds during torture sessions). Suddenly, I heard the sound of the *cravache* smack the ground.

"Take this dog out of here! He's useless."

The group of agents left and the Hadj rushed me to my cell, holding onto my arms and dragging my legs along the ground. I was prepared to prolong my time anywhere else—in the toilet with its awful smell, in the torture chamber with its whips and all manner of sadism, in this cement corridor—as long as I didn't have to go back to the cell where that hole, my fear, and the mouse were waiting for me.

13

The fear that lurked there and awaited me when I entered the cell was not the same as what I felt when I entered the torture chamber. My entire body shivered uncontrollably as I was thrown inside. Come, Mama. Come look at your son now.

The Hadj locked the door. I stood there whimpering in a strangled voice. All this torture and it's this mouse that looms as large as an elephant. I imagined that if they knew of my fear of the mouse and my complete collapse before it, they would organize a celebration for intelligence units worldwide. The upper echelons of these organizations would review their programs and give supplementary lessons to their units aimed at seeking to find the weaknesses of any given detainee. Just as we were able to drive Haydaoui, the carpenter, out of his mind when we were little, just by uttering the word "honey" which we would lob at him as we ran away. Like we used to drive Abdelghani crazy, making him laugh hysterically by tickling him on his sides or under the armpits. As for me, it was enough for them to throw me in with a mouse. I didn't know how far that would drag me.

As I mulled these fears over, I realized that I was still standing. I stretched out a little on the floor. I sat with my legs out in front of me. I put my hand on the ground and leaned my head back against the wall. No sooner did I position myself than I sensed a movement. I jumped up. I fixed my gaze on the hole, my eyes shooting out like darts. I crouched down and stayed there, alert as a shepherd afraid a wolf might get into his sheep's pen. Then it appeared. That's right, it appeared, but I had neither the power nor the strength to face it. Even if I did possess such courage, I was barefoot. I didn't have a shoe to stomp on it with. I remained crouching. It came out and began to poke around its hole. It wasn't silver-grey as I had seen it the first time, and as I had come to know it. I held my breath lest the slightest movement change it back to its silver-grey color and make it turn toward me. It continued to walk to the middle of the cell which I had, for so long, considered so small. But now it made me consider it in terms of corners, a middle, and sides. It got to the middle and stopped. I waited for it to move, continuing to hold my breath, silent. It balled itself up right there, tracing a circle in the middle of the floor and sitting down as if performing some kind of yoga moves. I swallowed my breath once again, nearly bursting with laughter. Would Youssef ever believe that I had sat face to face with a mouse? It moved a little, then returned to where it had come from without bothering me at all. Oh God, what had it discovered? Come on, come here. Could you leave me alone? Or could we become friends? I was speaking with it in a voice that was barely audible.

I told it that the reason for my unease, that my fear of it stemmed from the time when it bit my father's hand, the neighborhood holy man, the *fqih*. He had put his hand into the hole next to the bench where he kept his Qur'an. I was studying with him at the Qur'an school. He had sat me in the first row. He pulled his hand out from the hole and threw the Qur'an aside. Blood flowed from his finger and the other kids screamed in pain for their *fqih*, my father. The grocer, Bajloul, came and killed the mouse. When he saw how frighteningly pale my father had turned, he warned us that it was not a normal mouse, that it was rabid. This was confirmed with a visit to the neighborhood clinic. I had to hate you. It was the first time I ever saw weakness in my father, the first time his horse—a golden-armored horse—had ever stumbled. Despite subsequent lessons in natural sciences confirming that rabies is not found in all mice, time did what it did. This problem with all mice, or should I say against them, was enough to drive me crazy. Now you appear nice enough, as if cast from another mold entirely. Perhaps the mice of the 1950s are different from those of the 1970s. Twenty years or more is surely enough to change a person, to subjugate him, even to melt and re-form him entirely. Why can't the same be true for a mouse?

I glanced at it again. It could not have weighed more than the smallest starling. It was a faded grey, the color of dirt. Its eyes like grains of salt, their color impossible to determine. Its mouth and nose were two dots at the end of a straight line.

Only now will we make up. Perhaps we'll even become friends. It stirred where it was. No! It's not just a matter of getting to know one another and making up. I'm going to name you. I'll find a name for you. Yes, we've made up, but I don't think the matter of getting to know one another will be done in a day, at least not on my end. I know your kind. If it weren't for the other animals, you wouldn't be here living and breathing. Only after the ark had filled with dung and everyone complained about the filth to Noah did he squeeze the elephant's tail causing a male and female pig to fall from it, and they proceeded to eat all the manure. And when the male pig sneezed, you two—you and your female counterpart—came out. It follows, then, that were it not for the pig's sneeze, you wouldn't exist. I'll find a name for you so that any time I say it, you'll know I mean you. But what shall I name you? What shall I name you after all this fuss, after we've given in to one another, or at least I've given in to you? What?

I've got it! I'll name you Slimane Fuss, and why not?!

That's how my relationship with Slimane began, and that's how it developed in ways I didn't expect it to. After the trial began, they put us in an old wing that had been designated by the colonial administrators for prisoners connected to the nationalist movement. That day, I waited for Slimane to come out, once things had returned to normal. The mouse kept sliding toward its hole, only to come out again, kept disappearing and reappearing. No one expected that Slimane Fuss would jump to the top of the list of detainees, that he would spur the reinterrogation of all the comrades in order to find out who he was. It was his name I yelled out when the interrogators were coloring my flesh with their handiwork. My torture continued for many more days. Perhaps Slimane would sense how long

16

I was gone for and leave, never to return, so I yelled his name without meaning to. I didn't think about the lines of blood on my body when the interrogator stopped whipping me, and one of them yelled in my face,

"That's what you said yesterday! Who's Slimane? Is he the head of the organization? Is he the one who formulated the special document saying that Kida shouldn't be annexed? Tell us, who is Slimane?!" They went back to punching me in the ribs. I felt a fire consuming my joints, followed by an icy coldness, so I repeated the full name.

"Slimane Fuss."

They took me back to my cell where Slimane was sitting in the middle of the floor, clear as a headline gracing the front page of a daily newspaper. I saw him and smiled. All units would start looking for Slimane, and he was sitting right here. It took no more than a day and a half for their special intelligence apparatuses to verify that this name could not be located on any map in the country, among the living or the dead. It had never occurred to me before that mice might have been responsible for mapping the country, unless it was of a species specific to colonization. They took me and read more than twenty names that resembled Slimane Fuss—Ahmed Slimane, Ashour Slimane, Slimane Aicha—and I would assure them that I knew him by one name only: Slimane Fuss.

"Have you met him?"

"Yes! But no more than four times."

They wanted a description of him, so I gave them Slimane's precise features: small, slight, thin. Dirt-colored. Squinty eyes. With a mouth and nose smaller than a grain of wheat.

"Was he wearing glasses?"

"I don't know. He wasn't wearing them when I met him. Maybe he wore them other times for reading."

"Did he come see you alone, or was he with someone?"

"The four times we met, there was a woman with him."

17

"Same woman?"

"No."

Slimane seemed vague and general. That's all they got out of me. My case file was closed so they could open up a search for the comrade who went by the nom de guerre of Slimane Fuss. When they started to group us together in one wing, we were heartened that the trial was beginning, but it was a sad day for me because of my separation from Slimane. He went into his hole and didn't come out again. I dragged my legs slowly toward the open door of the cell. I looked back like a lover who sets a meeting with his beloved in a specific place, only to find that the morality police had come to make sure he knows that standing there was forbidden. I kept turning back toward the hole as I walked away, hoping that he might reappear.

2

DESPITE HAVING BEEN GROUPED TOGETHER in one cell block, there was nothing indicating that there was a trial on the horizon. The conditions in garde à vue, or police custody, were bad, too. From a purely theoretical standpoint, as garde à vue detainees, we were considered innocent because the authorities charged with issuing an innocent or guilty ruling hadn't done their job. From what we could gather from how we were being treated, the authorities seemed to despise us. What distinguished the garde à vue period was how harsh it was, how both local laws and international treaties were disregarded. And to top off all those violations, there was a total lack of medical care. Most of the illnesses we suffer from to this day are the result of that period and the conditions we faced while in custody. Our lawyers were not allowed to contact us. We were held in garde à vue for more than six months, which is what prompted us to go on a hunger strike demanding that we either be brought to trial or be released. After seventeen days on strike, they gave us their word that we would stand trial, which began after they tacked on an additional charge for all of us: exerting pressure and insulting the judicial apparatus, which came as a result of the message we had directed at the minister seeking action on our demands!

We thought the beginning of our trial would grant us the right to expose all these violations against us. We were betting on being able to reveal everything, starting with our having been picked up by unidentified persons in the street, in full view of our students at the schools where we taught, or in our workplaces. They didn't hesitate to break into our homes late at night. And as soon as they nabbed one of us and threw them—blindfolded and bound—into the unmarked car, the beating, torture, and insults would start and continue until we arrived at the unknown station. That is how we came to spend between four months and two years in the Derb Moulay Cherif secret prison. We had to lay on our sides or our backs. We were only allowed to sit up for short periods of time to eat—one meal a day—and every time we broke that rule, we were whipped. Blindfolds covered our eyes, and our hands were always bound. We were not allowed to speak, and only did so on the sly. To this day, I don't understand why they tortured us so much since we would be forced to sign our confessions without knowing what we had been charged with anyway, without them even untying our hands or removing the blindfold. The policeman would make us sign. One look at our signatures, which all looked the same, and you would know that they were the signature of one man, the policeman who guided our hands over the paper.

The conditions that accompanied our appearance before the representative of the public prosecutor and the investigating judge were always the same. One of our torturers in the secret prison would lead us into the office. The prosecution's investigation was just for show. It would begin with our being asked our name, profession, and place of residence. And it would conclude with a reading of the charges as laid out in the criminal investigative reports which were beyond anything we could have imagined. It was the same with the investigative judge, except that he would inform us that we were free to answer his questions, or we could hold off answering until the lawyer arrived. Immediately following that, the bandana would be retied over our eyes and our hands were bound again for us to be led to cars that would take us back to the prison.

That is how we held onto the notion of a trial like a drowning person clings to a bunch of straw when the presiding judge rejected all of our requests for substantive, incidental, and even superficial defenses. The focus was on our intellectual choices, and we were surprised when Ahmed Choufan was interrogated about his significant interest in foreign radio broadcasts. This was based on police reports that accused him of listening to a broadcast of France Inter that had held a symposium on the Kida region. Although all that had been established in our case was that we had formed secret associations and had printed and distributed leaflets encouraging people to demonstrate, they were all misdemeanor charges. What jumped up to the top of list of charges stacked against us was the charge of attempting to overthrow the regime and conspiracy to undermine state security.

A strong cordon consisting of various branches of armed forces and police was deployed around the courthouse, and even extended into the courtroom itself. Only a small group of family members was allowed to follow the proceedings, while the police were allowed to come and go as they pleased. The courtroom was barely large enough for us, and the defense found it extremely difficult to get to their places because the police were occupying most of the space in the room. And beyond this, they used the room underneath the hearing room to place cables that would transmit and record everything we said live from the accused's cage. The trial proceeded and we were handed harsh sentences that ranged from five years to life. Sixty of us were sentenced to twenty years, twenty detainees were sentenced to thirty years, and ten were given life sentences. The rest received sentences ranging between five and ten years.

We were dumbfounded by these sentences, our families even more so. Having been put in prison, with our families not allowed to visit us up close, we considered undertaking another battle. They were standing in the *parloir* visiting room with three sets of barricading bars extended between us. Our situation was bad. They crammed us into a special wing after throwing us into old, worn-out grey uniforms. There seemed to be some sort of set of instructions that did not stop at whipping us, or choking us with water, or burning us with cigarettes and electricity, or converting all those numbers into sentences that they dumped on us. In fact, it went well beyond all of that to include general abuse and humiliation that would last for the rest of our lives.

We went without sleep for three days and nights. We examined our situation from every angle. We decided to go on a hunger strike. There was no disagreement on what form it would take. We were still packed in as tight as the teeth of a comb. We went on an open-ended hunger strike which everyone passionately embraced in protest of the series of endless humiliations we faced. Even the nature of the sentences was a lump that remained lodged in our throats.

It was a day in June. The conditions didn't help. Everyone else was done with their final exams—unemployment knocking at the door—travelling and taking time off from work . . . But we had no other option when they served us a lunch of lentils that were hard as stones. We chanted poetry and slogans, still pulsing with enthusiasm. They removed the bowls of lentils just to make sure we were really on a hunger strike. We formed a discussion committee. We were ten comrades. During the third week, the Commander (that's what we had called him since our arrival at the prison) summoned us, and all ten of us stood in front of him so he could scream in our faces,

"The discussion's with one of you, not ten!"

The meeting did not produce even the most modest result. For half an hour, he continued to launch a single command.

"Break the strike!"

And when we stood our ground, he screamed in our faces,

"Take 'em to the prison wing to die. This country's full of other young people. If you had any good in you, they wouldn't have thrown you in here for life. Get out of here. Die for all I care!"

We returned to the wing. We found our comrades standing there waiting for us. We told them what had been revealed to us at the meeting. They went back to where they had been before, each one wrapped in his blanket. Evening began to cast threads of darkness. Everyone was exhausted after having spent the day singing and chanting slogans. Everyone seemed to be in a state of lethargic fatigue, so we gave in to sleep early. We were so tired, we forgot all about how hungry we were.

After the fourth week, our faces grew increasingly pale and we talked less and less. We started to spend most of the day lying in bed. Most of us were exhausted and feverish. Our families learned about the strike from the guards, and they were the first ones to inform some of the newspapers. And so, the summer proceeded as we used up what remained of our strength that had already been sapped by years of torture in secret prisons starting with the DST (Direction de la Surveillance du Territoire), then passing through Derb Moulay Cherif to garde à vue detention. We were still eating hunger for lunch when the prison administration resorted to tossing us one by one into the *cachot* of solitary confinement in order to isolate us from one another and pressure us individually with the goal of breaking our resolve. They had declared psychological war, with everything that war meant. There weren't enough *cachots* for us, so the process was done piecemeal. The Commander came in and laughed in our faces, yelling over and over,

"So you're fasting, may God accept it! As for your friends, they broke the fast with the afternoon call to prayer, right on time in Rabat and Salé, not a minute sooner or later."

Chuckling, he took a step back. As soon as he finished speaking, one of his lieutenants informed him that one of the prisoners was in critical condition.

"He's slipped into a coma. In fact, he might have d . . ."

The news hit us like a thunderbolt. The Commander couldn't hide his embarrassment, having barely just finished insulting our comrades. He rushed out and left us standing there. We went to the door and banged on it weakly, protesting with what remained of our hoarse voices. After a little while, we learned that the one who had slipped into a coma was Khalid, and that he had been transferred to the hospital on the prison doctor's insistence; otherwise, he would wash his hands of the whole affair because Khalid was in critical condition and could die at any moment. We no longer had the strength to speak, or even lift a finger. We started to completely deteriorate. But that didn't mean we let pass the opportunity to rush toward one another. We gathered, we came together as one, and we felt the loss together. We were dripping sadness and did not hide our tears. We wept that night and feared for Khalid.

Each of us fell into a coma, one after the other. Samad Mehdaoui was the only one who still possessed enough strength to slide over to us on his belly in order to place a damp piece of cloth on our foreheads. The hospital they transferred us to was not in the same city. The ambulances had to take us to the hospital in the capital, Rabat, because really, Gharbia is a dump of a city. It has few landmarks, the most important of which is the central prison.

I don't know how much time passed before we started to wake up from our comas. The first thing we did, as if it had been agreed upon ahead of time, was to remove the IV tubes. We were still steadfast in our battle and, having come this far, we could not stop now. Martyrdom or life! We weren't saying that it was a generous one, what with all those sentences that condemned us to living in prison, but we were betting on a life that was at least suitable for a political detainee. We learned from Nurse Bahija that we had been placed in two separate recovery rooms. We asked about Khalid and found out he was in the room next to ours. He had begun to recover slightly. The doctors and the rest of the health team were sympathetic to our condition. We could see that in their eyes as they constantly showered us with smiles. We asked Bahija if we could visit our comrades in the recovery room next to ours, but she refused. We pressed her but she stood her ground, so we decided to sneak in during the night to visit them anyway. The guards were posted at the main entrance to the recovery area, not in front of the two rooms.

The three of us—Youssef Mansour, Ali Ahrath, and I— tiptoed like children sneaking out, afraid their mother would catch them. We entered the neighboring recovery room which was draped in silence. We turned on the light, wanting to surprise our comrades. The lights had been off, but no one was sleeping. Their eyes were red and puffy. We were absolutely stunned by what we saw there and were all swept toward Khalid. I put my hand on top of his head, then on his forehead. He wasn't too hot. His eyes were pouring out sadness as he pointed with his finger. His eyes indicated that he wasn't pointing at me. He let the tears flow. Khalid wept along with all the other comrades as we wondered: what could be wrong?

There, close to the far edge of the room, one of the beds appeared to be empty. We asked again what was wrong, looking at each of the beds. Then, in a halting voice, Khalid replied,

"Samad Mehdaoui . . ." and he pointed to the empty bed.

"What about Samad? What happened to him?"

Everyone started crying and weeping again.

"May God have mercy on him."

"*Ya Rabb*! Samad. Samad . . . How? Why? When?"

We were shocked by the news which sent us to the ground in tears. We returned to the comrades in our room, unable to tell them about Samad Mehdaoui's martyrdom. Where would we begin? Who would believe that our sturdy hero had been defeated? But how could we hide what was in our eyes and our hearts? Where could we possibly conceal all that was choking us inside? Samad, Samad! The most composed one of all of us, and the last one to go into the hospital, had been vanquished by Death!

After Samad's martyrdom, we started talking. We wanted to push our demands as far as we could. Losing Samad was a huge loss, and nothing could replace him. We came to an agreement about all the demands we considered the most important and pressing. Salah Ribaoui commented,

"We should have added our release from prison to the list of demands."

But were there guarantees that our demands would be met? They began to allow our families to visit us at any time, and they met our demands for books, newspapers, and paper too. The visits made us happy as children. They told us about the battle they had waged during our detention and strike. It was a practical battle where they knocked on the doors of the prison administration, the Ministry of Justice, national, Arab, and international rights organizations, newspapers, and political parties. And they demonstrated at mosques too. We listened to how they had dispatched their troops and we couldn't believe it. Were these our mothers, sisters, and fathers? Were these our families from whom we had hidden our experience and our movements only to then place them face to face with this reality? It seemed to us that the principle of secrecy applied only to our families, families that towered like cypress trees.

I no longer recognized Mama. She told me about her movements with the families, about her confrontations with the police and the prison guards that had blown up into a full-scale war. Every time one of them said the word "prisoner," she'd yell in their faces,

"My son isn't a prisoner. My son is a political detainee!"

We had started to get up out of our beds when the order came for our transfer from the hospital back to the prison, which we opposed. The doctors insisted we stay, so we stayed four more months. The loss of Samad Mehdaoui was still fresh. We observed the forty-day mourning period for him there in the hospital while all the families went to his house, just as they had done when he was martyred. Lalla Aicha told us about how the house and surrounding alleys filled up around his mother. Family and friends came from all over the country as soon as they received news of his death. The neighbors were shocked when they realized all these processions filling the alleyways were for Samad.

"So then, Samad was pure." That's how one of the neighbor-women put it, so that all the neighbors would open their houses to us. Everyone spent the night in the alleyway where Samad Mehdaoui's house was.

Our presence there was strong, and all the neighbors' solidarity and how affected everyone in the city was provided a real support for Samad's mother and his wife, and for us as well. As for the body, the authorities refused to hand it over until Lalla Aziza (Samad's mother) or Kenza (his wife) signed something promising that no one would walk behind it. We pressured the family just to sign it and stay inside. That way, they could not be held responsible for whoever walked in the street and joined the funeral.

"Despite all the crying and sadness, we didn't feel like we were at a regular funeral. Rather, it felt like a bona fide wedding, even *more* than a wedding. They carried Samad's bier on their shoulders and human rivers surged in a procession the likes of which my eyes had never seen before."

Lalla Aicha sat recounting all the details, with us gathered around her as if she were a grandmother telling the very first story. Only when the salty tears reached our lips did we realize we were crying. This woman knew how to recount even the smallest details. She drew us in. We were transfixed and hung on her every word for more than three hours. We loved Lalla Aicha, as we did all the mothers. Lalla Aicha's mere presence among the families bestowed a special scent to everything. She told us about what she had said that so stunned the agents who came looking for her oldest son, Hassan. She was worn out, shocked as a result of Khalid's arrest, when she caught them off-guard with a kick and a scream as she pointed at her breasts.

"Why do you come now that I can no longer bear children? Khalid wasn't enough for you? Now you come for Hassan? The problem isn't with my children. The problem is with this milk they drank, right here. I've got anger and hatred for you here in my milk. But I'm going to burn this IUD and give birth to twins now! Nothing but twins!"

The families told us all of that, and we pressed Lalla Aicha to repeat it word for word, just as she had said it to the agents. She smiled and did just that. The words flowed from her lips like well-aged wine. This woman never went to school, never carried books under her arm, and knew nothing of poetry or the canon of the ancient Arabs. She hadn't read the works of Mahmoud Darwish or Mu'in Bsisu. She knew nothing of Samih al-Qasim or Mourid Barghouti. Nonetheless, the words she used were like theirs and brought to mind the loftiness of these poets who pulsed in our veins and who drove our every plaintive moan. The thing we felt in all its awfulness was the question of why all that secrecy around these lofty trees, our families? These trees that stood strong. She described how the procession had set out on foot from the alley, the martyr wrapped in the Palestinian flag and adorned with roses, with the sound of ululating following behind. From how she told it, I couldn't tell if it was hundreds or thousands of people, but it was a sea of humanity. Lalla Aicha laughed as if just realizing something, and said,

"Picture it. Now we've seen it all. We've seen women walking in a funeral. They told us that if we walked, the body might fall from its bier, or its shroud might tear, or the grave might not be the right size. But now we've seen it all. The first funeral we've ever walked in. The martyr didn't fall and the grave wasn't too small for him. We didn't wail and we didn't scream. We ululated as we raised our fingers up in a victory sign."

Right then I remembered Mama raising the victory sign as we entered the courtroom. She was trying to communicate with us using the same gesture I was. She raised her three fingers as I continued to look at her, pointing in her direction. She looked at me like an embarrassed child as she kept trying to arrange the fingers on her left hand with her right; too few fingers here, too many there. She kept staring at my hand, arranging and rearranging her fingers, until the victory sign rose up.

We left the hospital and went back to the prison to find that they had divided the wing up into individual cells where they had placed new beds and covers. This after having achieved our demand of being able to keep our own clothes, and being supplied provisions. We took charge of distributing them amongst ourselves and sharing the cooking duties. At first, we were enthusiastic about eating communally. That is, until the onset of many health issues stemming from the hunger strike made it necessary for each group to fend for itself. Then, for other reasons, the groups dwindled in size to two prisoners, and then even to just one.

Symptoms of stomach problems such as sores and lesions appeared in the majority of comrades, so it became necessary to follow a dietary regime. We were getting all our supplies from the prison administration and distributing them according to who needed what. We established an organizational chart for our lives there which included a Nutrition Committee, a Library Committee, a Presentations Committee, a Sports Committee, and so on.

All the committees worked assiduously and intensively. I was a member of the Library Committee that presented the prison administration with lists of our needs, from books of a theoretical nature to poetry and novels. We were determined to devour as many books of poetry and novels as we could, without knowing why. We went through a great many novels and at the time, we didn't have more than one copy of each. Tuesdays and Thursdays were set aside for returning and exchanging them, but due to increased demand, we eventually had to designate four days each week. As for the Presentations Committee, it set aside Mondays and Saturdays: one day for a cultural presentation and the other for a political presentation. As for the other days of the week, each of us was free to spend it as we pleased. And seeing as we had all decided to cling to the right to an education—those who were still studying as well as those who would re-register in other specializations—we needed to set aside some time for that to be established as well. Many talents presented themselves too, especially drawing. Abid would sit all day in front of his pictures where blackness and bars strongly integrated themselves into all his drawings. For his part, Salah Ribaoui devoted all his time to honing his poetic talent. A week wouldn't go by when I wouldn't find Salah running after me with a new poem. They were distinguished by their length, but they maintained a clear melodic rhythm throughout. Salah put great effort into constructing them and could not be convinced that he was done with a poem until almost six months had passed, with him chipping away at it from beginning to end. He was in no hurry. He would run after each of us in the prison yard, one after the other, until we had all read his poem and he had recorded our observations. I always used to tell Salah,

"You know I love your annual reports on Yemen or Japan, but you are a master of recitation. I consider it an essential element of the poem."

"You mean the art of delivering the poem."

"Of course. Our poets don't lack for imagination or imagery. But we love Mahmoud Darwish, Mourid Barghouti and Adonis more when we listen to them on cassette tapes, or hear them live."

The prison administration didn't provide us with the entire collection now held in the library; most of what we needed was brought by families, friends, and people who sympathized with us. We still made sure to visit the hospital, specifically to see Khalid who had emerged from his hunger strike severely weakened. The central nervous system, which coordinates and controls the body's functions, is located inside bone casings that effectively ensure its protection from external shocks, and the brain is the organized center for all functions, from feeling and movement, to memory and intellectual capacity. So, as the doctor described it to us, the membranes that surrounded the brainstem had not been fully formed or developed when Khalid began his hunger strike, which meant that they had suffered basic damage, reflected in the weight he lost. He could no longer keep still because of how much he trembled and shook. He had to see medical specialists constantly. Everything was damaged from his teeth to his vision to his ability to walk. Khalid remained a buried wound that all of us carried together in sadness. We talked about him in lowered voices when he wasn't around, and kept quiet about him when he was, to the point where all we could do was smother him with our affection. His condition was particularly serious as compared to others that generally caused relatively milder symptoms such as stomach ulcers, hemorrhoids, and weak vision.

Life in prison started to take on a familiar rhythm. Outside of our families' visits, the stress began to bear down hard on our psyches, and some strain in our relationships as comrades began to show. After seven years, it took on a bitterness that broke into different groups whatever unity our experience had known. Each group became a stand-alone entity, and each one began to provoke the other.

Discord began to emerge within the Presentations Committee. The theoretical presentations didn't cause any major arguments at first. However, when it became necessary to consider how to evaluate how things were going, it seemed that the majority was unprepared to listen to the romantic assessment that framed the experience as completely sacred.

We needed an objective assessment first. Dissecting our experience and identifying some of its weak points was necessary. This riled up some of the comrades enough for them to draw their weapons, and all we were left with was a rerun of trial after trial.

The seventh anniversary of Samad Mehdaoui's martyrdom was approaching, and it was that which ended up bursting our blisters. An announcement and program were posted in the library, but on the night of the memorial, we were shocked that two groups, which made up almost half of our number, were not there. We were extremely embarrassed by the absence because the memorial for Samad Mehdaoui, who knew nothing of our disputes, should have been bigger than all of that. Nonetheless, we stayed up late carrying out the program in its entirety. The following day, we ran into the comrades from the two absent groups in the yard. They were embarrassed, regret filling their eyes. Some of them hid from us so as to avoid our eyes meeting at all. Thus, the bonds that had been holding us together were starting to tear apart, which everyone outside the prison sensed when our communiqués began to come out signed by each individual group.

3

I DIDN'T KNOW THAT LEILA had separated from Mohammed and I only found out that she had spent two years in
the municipal prison after she surprised me with a visit. Leila
started to visit me regularly after Mama had been bearing the
brunt of that by herself. Leila started to alternate with her,
and because the central prison was only an hour from Leila's
work by train, she came regularly, at least twice a week. After
that, she convinced Mama to visit just once a month because
traveling such distances was bad for her health. So, Leila came
to visit me in prison, which started to both ease some of its
brutality (relatively speaking) and compound its viciousness
when the connection between us deepened.

Prison wasn't the only place that brought Leila and me
together. We had both belonged to the same framework—
she by way of her sympathies and I as a member—before
I joined the secret organization. I had always imagined her
as an organization person until it was confirmed for me two
years before I left the party that she had not been among its
members for a single day. But how could all of that energy
continue to float around outside of the organization? Really.
Why did she seem to be so much a part of the organization
when, in fact, she was so ephemeral, like water in the palm of
a hand? My relationship with Leila had been strong ever since
the students' conference that led to the boycott of the organization. What first drew me to her was her calm and her depth.

The discussions I had with Leila could not be had with any other woman. We had intellectual discussions as equals, discussions I only had with some of the other comrades. Despite how many women joined the movement, I don't know how I noticed her, or how the relationship between us deepened, at least on *my* part.

Mama's visits were essential to my survival, and Leila's visits became the force that improved the conditions of that survival. Leila was a force, there was no escaping that. Mama would arrive before it was time to go in. She would have to leave our city at eight in the morning to arrive at one in the afternoon and then wait out in front of the prison gate. She would come dragging a large basket loaded with all the essentials. I imagined her starting to put it all together from the time she said goodbye at the end of one visit until she came for the next one. And I would prepare for her arrival by aging the milk, frying the potatoes, and airing out the mattress we would sit on in the corridor. Mama considered these in-person visits extremely beneficial. When our disappearance went beyond twenty months, Mama only asked for one thing, which was to see me alive, but now she says,

"Now I can grab you and touch you and hug you. Praise be to You, my Generous God."

She touched me as if she couldn't believe I was there. She came bearing kisses and greetings from family and neighbors, as well as the fragrance of the city that I still carry here in my nose. The broken pole still stood at the end of the street, as did the daghmous tree that provided some shade in front of the house. There were potholes, the potholes all over the alley that filled with water in the winter and grew bigger in the summer. And the children were exactly the same as they always were. Their favorite thing to do was to gather in front of our doorstep. The only difference was that I was no longer the one responsible for gathering them there. Not much to add, except that Bajloul's death made me feel as if the broken electrical pole had fallen over completely. The only pole I liked to lean on. I would lift my right foot to touch the pole's steps, leaving the other foot flat on the ground. And when my legs got tired, my body would carry them to Bajloul's shop, where a few goods were lined up on the shelves and a steady stream of regular customers came and went. It was there where I learned by intuition that lessons aren't necessarily only taught in school, when Bajloul said that philosophy is a mute woman, and that poetry is a boy who speaks on her behalf. I used to imagine everything he said was authoritative, so I would never need to tell. I was thirteen years old when I headed to his store to pick up a can of tomatoes. It was two in the afternoon. The door to the shop was half open. I raised the counter up after hunching and leaning over a little bit so I could sneak in, in case he was sleeping. I was walking on tiptoes when I surprised him as he ate. In the middle of Ramadan! He ate as if it was just another lunch. My mouth hung open. I turned toward him, and he continued to eat, inviting me to join him and showing no concern at all. After finishing, he handed me a can of tomatoes. He recorded it in his notebook and I left, turning back to look at him and hoping he would ask me not to reveal the secret. Something I didn't understand for five years when I went to his store throughout the month of Ramadan.

"Bajloul died. He thought a lot about you."

That's how Mama told me about the death of a man who never went to school, but who was an open book, full of pride. Bajloul died and in him, something in me died too. He never visited me in the central prison, but his greetings always came at the top of the list of greetings that Mama delivered, as did his many gifts of food that she brought in her basket. Bajloul never married. No children or family. But those who loved him flocked to him from all around to distribute the spoils. That's how Mama would always bring me back to my childhood. When we would meet in the corridor, memories from childhood would be intense and sustained—our relationships before prison, my rowdiness, various places I remembered. I would ask her about the alleys, the streets, the lake; trying as hard as I could to grab onto my memories so as not to completely forget. You had to renew the images, not with the eye, not by touch, but rather, through storytelling. Mama would narrate and I would imagine the details. I didn't understand why she continued to wear the white mourning clothes she had worn after father's death and then after the end of the mourning period, which came no more than two weeks before I was arrested. I only understood when Lalla Aicha told me when I was in the hospital. I was suffering from dizziness, then nausea. My blood pressure felt like it was rising rapidly. The unfortunates arrested Mama (who had been in mourning clothes for a full week) to find out who had gone into the house immediately following my arrest to clear out the books and private papers from the library. She cried and confirmed that she thought it was one of the agents. The families gathered when news got out and they went to her, to gather in front of the police station, filling the area with protest.

"They threw us out. They spit in our faces. They falsely accused us. And then they released Lalla Cherifa."

That's how Lalla Aicha told it. And that's how Mama explained why she continued to wear mourning clothes.

"Not out of sadness for my husband, nor for my son. Rather, out of sadness for my country that didn't respect my grief."

I didn't know anything about it until after Mama left, and I longed for her next visit like a baby crawling toward its mother's breast. I felt a loss like no other and when she finally came to me in the hospital, I embraced her tightly, begging her forgiveness. So, she knew that I knew. When we got back to the prison, we had to contact all the political and legal parties and bodies, and we had to write to all the newspapers to expose the injustices that our families had been subject to. As for Leila, she was the bridge between the heart and the mind.

She would come carrying newspapers and any new publication that discussed recent political developments. Over the period that she visited me in prison, Leila changed a lot from how I had known her before, even though hints of something had been there for all to see. I was constantly putting off trying to catch her, because once you caught this woman, she would just slip away again. Leila would slip away like water from the palm of your hand, or like air you won't be able to breathe in a second time, or like a wave you can't dive into twice. Leila's visits were like one of those practical training sessions that had no more than two members. Leila was the lily of the soul, and I was the sad desert thorn.

4

WE HAD TO DEVELOP OUR financial resources in order to cover our book and nutritional needs. We were trying to forge a sense of stability, each in his own way, to preserve something of a balance that none of us would hesitate to admit didn't exist inside the darkness of prison. Provisions had started to dwindle, especially after the administration noticed that our group was splintering. We weren't even standing in solidarity with battles on the outside. The principle of solidarity was there but coming up with a way to embody it differed from one group to the next, especially after each group in Gharbia had started to extend into other prisons following the arrests that came on the heels of the most recent strikes, just as they found their way into the student sector.

The situation was bad in the other prisons, unimaginably horrible, in fact. We learned about it through reports from families and news of their protests in the newspapers. The open-ended hunger strike resulted in martyrs, but not in achieving actual gains. The security apparatuses hid the rest of the detainees who insisted on continuing with the strike until they too achieved martyrdom. They have disappeared to this day. Fate unknown. Only one of them turned up later, damaged, as if he had been hit by a bomb.

The country started to see the appearance of human rights organizations and our case began to rise to the surface and gain more traction after a period when our arrest had practically convinced everyone that this all was normal and natural. In fact, some of us were almost convinced of this too. The comrades' ten-year sentences had ended. We formed a procession with them as we walked to the prison gate, hugging one another like children who had discovered each other for the first time. They started to gather their things and hand them out.

"Take this sweater, Mouline. It's cold in here." "These papers and pens are yours, Salah. You'll need them." "And these socks are for you, Ahmed. Be sure to keep your legs and joints warm. The rheumatism mustn't reach the heart." And so it went until they had gotten rid of all their things and stood either with their hands in their pockets or embracing us.

We went with them as far as the prison gate. We stood inside calling out their names and cheered their freedom until the gate opened and the families' trilling and calls reached us. They went out to them, and we went back to ourselves, to our cells, dragging our feet and chewing on our pain bit by bit so as not to allow it to fall onto our hearts all at once. We went back to our cells and curled up like nobodies, worn out by the anguish of prison. Only Leila was able to break through some of the darkness, and I was like a leaf that flutters before falling, with nothing holding it to the tree branch save for two threads: Mama and Leila. I swung from one to the other, nursing longingly from Mama's bosom and drinking the wine of love that poured from Leila's breast. What would things have been like had Leila not split up with Mohammed? I'll tell you this: one man's loss is another man's gain.

The years were able to forge many relationships between us and the prison guards, which allowed some of us to be released to the hospital to meet up with our girlfriends. I would alternate between visiting the dentist and the eye doctor, just to meet with Leila outside the space of the prison. But for all those years, we could only meet inside the prison or the hospital. Why only in these enclosed spaces? We'd shut ourselves in a small room in the hospital and I would embrace Leila with the thirsty heat of years, my body coming into contact with hers like teeth chattering from life's chill. When we began to demand that we be able to receive our wives and girlfriends in our cells for part of the visiting time, the Commander grinned from ear to ear as he scattered the newspaper pages in front of us and tossed us the one with Abdelfattah Fakihani's article "Our Right to Love" on it. Even though everyone was living this loss, Group A's reaction was to disapprove of the article because it sought to preserve its hollow pride. The important thing was for us to reflect a peak of resilience that we no longer possessed. Deprivation and loss developed and spread like a cancer eating away at all of us. I didn't understand why this group was so adamant in its rejection of personal and natural rights. How can you imprison yourself, inside a prison?

I remember when the wife of Boujemaâ (one of the heads of Group A) asked for a divorce. It happened right when we got to prison and were sentenced. He got a life sentence. I remember we talked about it for a month. Of the women we were involved with, some didn't know a thing about our experiences, and others didn't have more than a superficial knowledge of what went on inside the student movement, except for the female comrades who were also arrested and were now in Ismail Prison or in the women's ward here in Gharbia. We didn't try to imagine the conditions these women faced after we were arrested. News of our arrests came as a shock and the sentences crashed down on them like mountains that the wind could not budge. Boujemaâ needed to come to terms with this, but fiery anger shot out of his mouth in a river of insults and attacks on his wife. The situation of married couples was worse than that of those who had left girlfriends at school or in lecture halls at the college, or whose dates were left waiting for them, never to show up, after their arrests. Even though we were convinced that being arrested was the price we had to pay for our principled convictions, deep down, we were still counting on the women to share the burden with us. We all dreamed of a woman who would pull us out of the darkness toward a light that would shine inside the prison gloom. It didn't matter that the candle was burning. What was important was that it provides light for us in prison, even if just in a corner of our cell where you sought refuge to paint it yellow so the light would seem brighter. Leila was my light, but she refused to be a mere bridge to cross . . .

"When will you all see us as people in and of ourselves rather than as mere bridges over which you can escape the darkness when you're thrown into prison? And upon release, we become nothing more than a boat for crossing the night. And then, there might be many boats. But the root of it is in what you picture us to be. Your perception which dwells right here."

Leila reaches her fingers to the back of my head and then brings them around to the front. I grab onto her fingers and put them back again.

"If the perception, as you say, resides here, then we have nothing to do with it. The skull was inherited from our forefathers, and we aren't responsible for how it's arranged."

I tried to move Leila away from a subject I knew we were still unable to delve into at length, but Leila's earnestness stopped my glibness in its tracks.

"The problem, Mouline, is that women develop so fast, even *you* all can't absorb it. After ten years have gone by with you here in prison, and after your assessments of the experience, there's no getting around the basic fact that the country also needs to struggle for these small things. You've laid down a plan that seeks societal change and you've underlined it with a thick red pen. At the same time, you've lowered the curtain on social issues that knock on our hearts every day. Why don't we start with these things that remain obscured by the curtain, these seemingly small things? Women, housing, corruption, education . . . These battles require daily and heroic struggle. In fact, they constitute democracy when transformed into a societal pursuit. We're not in a rush. We want to cleanse our country, but with water, not blood."

Unlike her usual self, Leila was talking non-stop, and I felt the weight of the approaching question. But she put off fencing me in. She paused for a moment, then continued.

"Could Boujemaâ, or any of you have waited for your beloved while she served a life sentence? Could he have done that? You know that there are women waiting for you with mystical devotion. Visit. Work. Home. Seriously, could you all do that?"

I should have jumped on this question, for I had embraced it many times without hiding the fact that I had acquired a certain flexibility in dealing with the issue whenever I took aim at it. I lit countless cigarettes throughout the night thinking about it, but found myself having to dodge the question, so I came up with a sarcastic response.

"Of course, these are things we acquire, and we can't free ourselves of the history of our acquisitions so easily."

"Good for you and your pale history."

"And good for *you* and your red history."

As soon as Leila heard my response, she burst out laughing and responded immediately,

"Red history! Meaning the history of menstruation?!"

Leila lifted her hand and gave me a high five as she guffawed. Leila still fills me up. As she supports me, she is my rock that shows me how much we're dying, bit by bit, inside a space such as this that increases its darkness within us. Whenever I think about Leila, Rajae, Nouzha, Souad, Assia, Najat, Rabia—women who do everything in their power so that *we* can continue living—I feel the weight of Leila's questions. Would we be able to squander our best years, moving from one point to the next only to arrive at a woman behind bars? Deep down inside I felt something being churned about through these women. This was a sign that could not pass just like that; this handful of women developing at a pace us men

43

hadn't absorbed yet. An image of a woman's boudoir was still buried inside us, here in the back of the head. How can all this consciousness be born all at once? Through Leila, I felt that women in this country were a sun that men were trying to burn so it wouldn't extend beyond the edge and burn *them*.

How can we comprehend something we say, as loudly as we can, that we had nothing to do with? Leila replenishes me. And whenever I think about her, or listen to her, or talk with her, I feel she is filling me up inside. Even the silence that so often surrounds her makes me whole.

5

OUR GROUP HAD STARTED TO publish a monthly magazine here
from prison which included some articles of an academic nature,
as well as creative works ranging from short stories to poetry,
as well as drawings and caricatures too. We tried to gather the
largest possible number of comrades around this project. Our
goal was not to fill the darkness of prison time, nor was it to
bring back the parts of our bodies that had been broken. We
only dreamt of creating a memory for us. True, we will pass
on from here despite the years piled up on our chests that draw
deep lines on our faces and cause white hairs to stick out of our
foreheads, but we will still possess something of the dream. We
had to write the history of the throbbing pulse of our lives here.

We disagreed somewhat on the name. All the suggestions tended to inflate the project, beginning with its name.
We didn't need to make it sound like a political slogan from
the get-go. We didn't know how much it could be embodied. It would be preferable for the magazine's subject matter
and material to convey the unexpected. We weren't aiming
to expose ourselves right from the start. That's why Salah
insisted that the magazine's name be very simple, fun even.

We rallied around Salah's suggestion and defended it.
The names that were suggested such as *Democratic Destiny* and
The Purpose took a back seat. *Ravency* emerged as the name that
would stick. We all exploded with laughter when Salah clarified the significance of the name and what it referred to.

All Gharbia really had in those days was a prison. Its most famous landmark at the end of the colonial era was the five-star Covency Hotel, the first of its kind in the entire country. It became a destination for those ravens wearing their Kufi caps, flying in from the Gulf, drawn to it at night by the sex that was available there.

Very quickly, the ravens transformed Gharbia into a brothel that attracted prostitutes as plentiful as breadcrumbs from all over the country. This is where Salah got the inspiration to name it *Ravency*, referring to the Covency Hotel. And it is what Abid would artistically depict on the magazine's cover where, over the word "Ravency," he placed decorative dots that resembled tears of protest dripping from the city's eyes (it was the least he could do). Then, all around the edges of the magazine's name, he drew one star for each of us, and put them in handcuffs. Our one hundred and thirty-nine stars seemed countless as compared to the five stars of the Covency that had been wrapped up in the wickedness of its time. We were as happy as children with their new holiday clothes when we finished preparing the first issue. We made sure everyone who visited that week left with a copy under their arm. It looked truly and surprisingly wonderful, and was encouraged by everyone, with friendly pens contributing to it from outside the prison as well. Thus, we would take on the burden of regularly publishing a magazine for three years. This would cause ripples on the outside, until the latest uprising that had resulted in the arrest of so many young people. Ultimately, *Ravency* would form the subject of our interrogations and torture, and a main charge in court. So it was inevitable that the project be forced to stop. I don't know why *we* are rounded up whenever a popular movement springs forth in this country. An uprising is the spontaneous expression of people who have been burned by high prices and, as a result, go out yelling into the streets and alleys, hunger gnawing away at their insides. They demand nothing more than survival, and *we* were demanding that the conditions of that survival be better. Thus, blood flows in the streets and *we* are taken so it can be wiped up with our flesh. *We* are thrown into prisons until the pools of blood dry up. I began to feel certain that this country was nothing more than one big prison. Cervantes tilted at his windmills all over the world, but he was only arrested when he got here, to the northern coast of this country. Henri Michaux's characters raised challenges from the start but when they arrived in Casablanca, the challenges fell under arrest. My Lord! How are fact and fiction so intertwined that our country is a space fit only for prisons?

Ever since we arrived at the central prison in Gharbia, we have become accustomed to so much of the Commander's bad behavior. Even if he was not to be seen sometimes for a week, he was sure to be there on Friday, sure to walk around the yard while we were here hung out to dry like laundry on the inside, just a stone's throw away from him. We began to grasp what he was up to. As soon as the clock struck eleven in the morning, the cassette tape would start and blare as if he had placed a loudspeaker to amplify the sound to reach all the wings of the prison. But *we* were the message's intended audience. The Commander could not change the tape the whole time he was in charge of running the prison. The Qur'an reciter had a melodious voice. But the Commander would not leave the tape to play from beginning to end. Rather, every time, he would insist on stopping the tape player and rewinding the tape at the same point in the chapter. It was Surat Yusuf, but the particular verse the Commander played was always the same. He would clasp his hands behind his back and walk toward us, turning here and there, wherever we were, chanting in his jarring voice,

He was good to me when He brought me forth from the prison, and again when He brought you out of the desert, after that Satan set at variance me and my brethren. My Lord is gentle to what He will.

The chanting he threw in our faces jolted us out of the languid state we were in. The Commander walked up to Salah and

47

took a look at what he was writing. He walked away from me as I sat in the middle of the courtyard basking in the sun. Abid was leaning on the door leading into the yard when he yelled out to Salah as he grabbed the door handle, slowly turning it with his hand. The handle was thick and rusty. Abid spelled out what was written on the back of the handle and laughed.

"Did you know this lock is made in China?"

In response, Salah shouted in a loud voice that pulled us all out of our stupors as he pointed to the Commander who was still looking at him and chanting his verses . . .

"And this Commander . . . he's made inside ya!"

We all burst out laughing at the rhyme which annoyed the Commander, and continued to snicker as his response came clothed in his usual accusation of apostasy.

The whole time the Commander was in charge of Gharbia prison, we heard every year from the guards that he had decided to perform the hajj pilgrimage to Mecca. But every time the date of the hajj approached, the Commander would start to backpedal until he had done a complete about-face. We didn't understand why until the guard, Allal, confided in us that the Commander just wasn't sure about airplanes, despite their tangible existence. His mind just couldn't accept them. Not to mention the fact that they were not mentioned in the Qur'an. Otherwise, he would just shut his eyes and throw himself onto one so he could undertake the journey and perform the hajj.

We had a good laugh about it, but his desire to visit Mecca persisted. Every year, word would come that he was going to perform the hajj, but as soon as the season approached, he would go back on his decision. He kept searching the Qur'an, poring over each sura, and examining every verse until he found it. His yelling reached us before he did.

"I found it! I found it!"

"Against you shall be loosed a flame of fire, and molten brass."

6

LEILA'S VISIT WAS APPROACHING SO I pulled myself up from under a sun that was working to loosen all my limbs. I don't know why I insist on bathing every Friday. Even if I were to bathe three times in a week, I would still find myself having to bathe again on Friday. I feel a giddiness on this day in particular, remembering those Fridays when my father would wake me up before dawn so we could head to the neighborhood hammam. This ritual used to frighten me. Waking up at dawn or even earlier to head to the hammam as if it were necessary to get rid of the ghosts in my dreams with hot water that flowed into my veins and seeped into my pores. It was only then that I started to become intimately familiar with the hammam. And because I had reached the age of ten and was still wetting the bed, my father insisted on waking me up every Friday before I did it, because Mama had convinced him that I only peed at dawn (so many times had she stayed awake at my side touching the bed until late at night checking to see that it was still dry). My father added that peeing in the wee hours of the morning was a deed that came from Satan's filth, until I came to believe that, were I to pee in the dead darkness of night, I would be performing an angelic act. So, once, I aimed to pee as soon as my head hit the pillow. My eyes open, I tried to squeeze them shut to create some of the sleeping rituals of peeing. I pulled my legs together and pressed on my penis so you couldn't hear the flowing pee. However, it turned out that peeing with the angels didn't replace peeing with Satan at dawn, and I woke up in the morning as if I had bathed in a pool of acrid water. This was enough for my father to visit me at school and drop a bomb on my head in front of the whole class. My teacher, Fatima Amine, called me to the front of the class where my father was standing. He reached his hand out to me and I was delighted. There was no way someone reaching their hand out to you like this would slaughter you in front of this crowd that had only known me for three months after having transferred from Ms. Ghiyati's to Ms. Amine's class. My teacher signaled with her eyes for me to stand up straight, and my father asked,

"Do you know this boy?"

They answered at the top of their lungs as if they had caught an easy question.

"Yes!"

"What's his name?"

They shouted even louder than before.

"Mouline Lyazidi!"

"Wrong. His name is *The Pisser* Mouline Lyazidi." The class exploded into a laugh that struck me like an arrow. I rushed back to my seat, avoiding the glares of the other students. Then, just like that, my father disappeared. Just as my name, Mouline, disappeared and was replaced by "The Pisser." Hamed, who sat next to me, began to act as if he were above sitting there, and every time I turned to him, he would pretend to be determined to change seats. I would shoot him a sympathy-seeking look that begged him to stay and not make matters worse. I was certain I wasn't the only one in the class who wet the bed, but my father had insisted on shaming me right here in the classroom. Before my father had showed up, I am sure no one had considered that I wet the bed. Mama would lose sleep so I would be clean each and every morning, dressing me in a way that impressed my teacher. But my father destroyed everything with his visit. The nickname was on all the students' lips, and not just in my classroom or in my grade, but even outside in the yard where more than one classroom came together. When I left the house for school, I had to pass by Bajloul's store to buy two riyals worth of *fanid* cookies and chocolate in order to bribe the students not to jeer me all day. Mostly what I remember after what my father did was that, whereas before I had been going to sleep early, now I guarded myself from getting any sleep at all, vigilantly denying myself even a wink of sleep that might drag me into pools of urine. The cost of all that water from me was very high indeed. First there was the initial scandal in front of the class. Then there was the changing of my name from two names to three— first name, family name, and a nickname – The Pisser – that lurked before the two other names, waiting to ambush me.

The lack of sleep was reflected in a distinct pallor and I began to lose my appetite which resulted in a weight loss of five kilos. During a visit to the doctor, Monsieur Guite, Mama explained the problem to the nurse who passed it on to the doctor and they had a good laugh together. He came up to me squeezing my shoulder, mussing my hair, and repeating my name, "Mouline, Mouline." I don't remember the details of the examination anymore, nor am I required to, but I remember well the prescription Monsieur Guite gave me that consisted of a dropper vial of something that might be credited with the beginning of the end of my bed-wetting. I began to regain my weight and my color came back. What I could not do, though, was get the students to stop making fun of me and temper their affection for calling me "Pisser" over and over again until I got up the nerve one day to ask my father to come to school and tell the students I no longer wet the bed at all, just like he came the first time. My father burst out laughing, squeezed my shoulder, and walked out saying,

"When you get older, you'll forget all about it."

I got to my cell, changed my clothes, and put on a dash of cologne that Leila had given me for my birthday. I had never celebrated my birthday before she came along. I even had to check my ID card to verify the day and month when asked. It was only Leila who got me to embrace it. I shaved my mustache. I splashed cologne on my face. That's what we're like when all we have is the inside, and grief for the loss of the outside world that we once had. Here, where we see our faces quite by accident in the eyes of a woman, we grow more convinced of ourselves. I gathered up my aired-out mattress under my arm and headed out to the corridor. Leila and I had made it a habit of sitting at the end of the hallway. It was a square corner separated from the corridor by some plywood, enough to serve as a barrier against prying eyes. Leila's Friday visits were conducted in the "mihrab niche of love," as the comrades liked to call it. As for her visits on other days, we would sit in the corridor, often hugging and kissing for all to see.

Prison awakened me, awakened many of us, in fact, to the little things we had overlooked, things that had seemed insignificant when we were on the outside. The way we looked. Our clothes. A love for life that now seemed to be little more than a square of sky visible from the prison yard. A love for the ocean as it quietly laps at my hand at night. Music. Women in all their particulars. Prison is savage loneliness. And it has the potential to become a deadly loneliness if the prisoner closes his eyes and does not dream of the ocean, or women, or wide-open spaces. Prison is twice as lonely when you put your hands into those of a woman when she visits, and you bury your nose in her hair, pass your mouth over the sides of her neck, kiss her all over her face, and breathe in deeply. And after a few minutes, the guard comes in holding a clock above his thick mustache to indicate that the visit is over. Prison is madness, no doubt about it. When time is closed off to you in its darkness, where neither dreams nor love can prop you up. Deeply held convictions cannot possibly stand on their own. Imagine anything inside an airtight bottle. Would it be possible to wait patiently for a lifetime even if this bottle were filled with perfume? The prison system and its mechanisms cannot be faced solely with doctrinal or political conviction and an optimistic view toward the future. It cannot be considered the basis that directs and organizes the resistance. It cannot be summarized by political conviction under specific conditions with common features such as routine, idle time, and exhausting oneself by digging holes inside a vacuum. Resistance requires a fully conscious response that feels this sacrifice, that brandishes all the weapons this confrontation serves. That is why, whenever we grabbed onto a book or a woman or something to rattle our memories, we bit into it as if settling an account with a front line that was bleeding us dry.

Leila arrived and I was eager to see her, but there seemed to be a hint of sadness on her face. I gave her a warm hug and she hugged me back twice as hard, as if she were hiding something she could only express through her grief and how strongly she hugged me. We sat. I asked her what was wrong. She tried to conceal her sadness. I insisted. I felt that she was distant, lost. Leila put her hand in mine, threw her head down onto my shoulder, and burst out crying. I had never seen Leila like this before. I had known her through the most painful and difficult situations, and Leila didn't cry. She didn't shed tears easily, but now she was crying, her eyes like gushing springs. Then she muttered some broken words through her tears.

"My dear Lalla Cherifa."

"Mama. What's wrong with her? What happened?"

Leila burst into tears again. I felt a heat rising up to my ears and a buzzing inside my head. I felt like a slaughtered bull. I insisted on knowing what happened.

"May God have mercy on her."

Leila kept crying so loudly it brought all the comrades out into the corridor. I didn't ask her for details. About how or when Mama died. I knew that she was suffering from rheumatic heart disease which had begun to cause paralysis below the waist. I hadn't seen her for six months but didn't imagine the illness had gnawed away so much at her that she would have died. I didn't ask about anything and sat in silence for the entire visit. Leila just stared at me and cried. Most of the comrades remained standing while some of them kneeled. Others lay on the floor. The silence was terrifying. They tried to break it with condolences and words of comfort, but words were old, and the time for talking was past.

I felt myself breaking apart into shards of grief. I didn't know what to do. I felt that saying anything was useless. Total silence, only when it is transformed into a fear that lowers its curtain over the eyes and the heart does it become the most eloquent form of expression. The scene had to end as soon as possible. This space only allowed me a few hours with Leila, in whom I might have released some of the roar of my yearning for Mama. The end of the visit was already approaching. I just wanted this scene to end so I could slink back to my seclusion and retreat into my burning longing for Mama. Perhaps my cell could lift some of this heavy weight bearing down on my chest.

Leila started to pull herself together enough to get up after the guard insisted that the visit was over. Her eyes were red from so much crying. She threw her head down on my chest, turned her face up toward mine, and hugged me. I placed my hand on her neck, held onto it warmly and took a step backward with a gesture that pulled her to me and pushed her away at the same time, an injunctive attraction. Leila was not expecting me to do that, but it had to be done to end the scene. I went back in, slowly dragging my feet toward my destiny. My cell seemed more oppressive than ever. Dear God, how could I be deprived of placing a farewell kiss on Mama's forehead? How could I be prevented from walking in her funeral procession and receiving condolences? I spent the night, the entire night, moaning and smoking cigarettes, but my tears found it difficult to fall. I felt their heat, but they stayed inside, falling onto my heart instead. I lit the first cigarette of the second pack from the last one of the first pack. I didn't need an ashtray or a lighter. I swallowed them like black pus.

Mama had been dreaming of my release from prison and was preparing for Leila's and my wedding day. I know, right here, in the folds of the heart that could not give her more time to live longer, that she wanted it to be a big wedding.

She was always playing with her small round prayer beads, never passing the fourteenth one before going back to the beginning and then pushing on as far as twenty beads. That's how Mama's fire went out. Oh, how my heart burns for this Mama!

Our experience was laid out before me by the harshness of our detention. The toll of an entire lifetime behind bars. An exorbitant price to pay for a handful of ideas. Is there a greater price than one's freedom? Losing those who are dearest to us without even so much as a goodbye kiss or a glance at the casket as it heads to the place of no return?

Leila came to visit me two days later. She was wearing a brown jilbab and had put a scarf over her hair. Sad. She seemed broken. The sadness she felt for me while I was in prison was even greater than her sadness for Mama. I felt this and understood it. However, when I directly broached the topic of the need for a new assessment of the experience, it surprised her, given how painfully serious being apart was. She didn't betray her surprise too much, but I could sense it in her eyes when she asked me,

"But why not have the assessment take the form of a written research study that might be published, for example, and not limit it to an oral assessment that might not be accessible enough to be useful?"

I was somewhat taken by the idea. Leila left and came back two days later. I had been mulling her suggestion over for two nights. Had the time come to blow things wide open? How long would we be dragged along to repeat something we continue to be revered for, duped from behind bars? Bearing the sacred totem had tired us out. We had to speak the shards of truth we had within us. The experience was no more

55

than a tattered rag of mistakes. Why shouldn't we say this collectively, after fourteen years in prison? Everyone knew, or at least admitted to themselves, what the fatal mistakes were. That's how some of the slogans such as "red foundations" or "every public battle has echoes in the university" started to lose their sheen. They reverberated, pounding in my ears, in all my pores. Can a person throw their entire life away for the sake of some slogans that cannot be considered even a reflection of our reality? The only thing we could be thankful for is that these seizures of doubt did not pounce on us during our torture and interrogation sessions inside the secret prisons. We had to hold ourselves together there.

Could the assessment have taken less than these fourteen years? Did we possess the courage that would make it possible for us to dig deep into our souls? Collective courage had not been possible before now. Today, the intimacy of prison and the graying of our hair as we stared up at the ceilings of our cells had, at the very least, born an individual courage in every one of us, even though differences about how we would express this courage would remain different from one individual to the next, and from one group to the next. But for the first time, I was ready to shout out at the top of my lungs: "Let's disagree publicly to show the people what we've agreed to in secret."

I dressed my musings in simple words, and questions began to present themselves to me: How could this new Left, that consists of us, build a foundation by harassing and viciously criticizing the national parties more than it does the regime? Why was the work of unification absent on a grand scale? And why does that work also become invigorated when it faces secondary contradictions, yet it fades when faced with the essentials? Could we coordinate with the political organizations we left after having entirely rejected them? And after all this time, who benefits from this situation? The regime, the parties, or the new Left? What any one of us can be sure of when they have their eyes closed is that the first loser is us, this

Left that only comes up with wind and dust.

Leila let out a few deep sighs and gave me a sharp look as she laid into me.

"You all are being consumed like stars on a moonlit night. Do you think that any experience can be 100% negative or 100% positive? Even if the experience doesn't yield any results, it's based on a gamble. Look at the human rights situation in our country and how people are now referring to it as national, Arab, and international all at the same time. Human rights, even though they begin with the matter of your imprisonment, aren't limited to it. Rather they extend to the rights of citizenship in general and they're what create democracy as an urgent social demand. I'm not at all prepared to listen to all this sobbing. Enough with the self-flagellation. Yes, you may have made mistakes like everyone else, but this doesn't rob you of your political purity."

"Do you consider the assessment of a specific experience to be a type of self-flagellation?"

"An assessment that's wrapped up solely in blackness can only be flagellation; even total destruction of the self, especially since you all are in prison and not on the outside. You need to search, even plunge into the positive elements of the experience in order to feel settled and calm inside. You desperately need these elements, few as they may be, and to avail yourselves of them, not deem them useless.

"My focus on the negative elements of our experience comes essentially from the charged atmosphere that surrounds us whenever we keep rushing toward this step at the comrades' insistence to formulate a literature of glorification. That's what I consider a part of the general problem. Of course, we don't have to pay attention to the fact that the periods of mass expansion and popular uprising the country has experienced have no connection with *us*, the Left. And there's no need to say it out loud. We knew more about Russia than we did about our own country. In our struggle, we didn't produce any knowledge of our own reality. Despite that, we dressed it in red without asking what *its* favorite color was. All we did was reduce proposals of the second Internationalism to local slogans, and we thought that was enough to impose revolution."

This is where the Left is. Everyone revived the one and only when they built their secret existential organization according to the model Lenin provided in his book *What Is To Be Done?*—his main argument for the Russian Revolution. We revived the one and only when we made Sir Marx into a prophet. We also established the primacy of *What Is To Be Done?* as a source of nothing more than a draft formulation of the question, and here we have given it an absolute answer.

Leila insisted again that I begin the assessment in writing and leave it open to relativism. In her view, the issue did not always fall on one of two sides, be it right or wrong, black or white.

She left, her questions and perfume continuing to waft around me. Leila is someone who cannot remain a mere observer. To talk about Leila, which I find nearly impossible to do, is to speak about a woman who can sow life in ice. Leila is a flame that never goes out. I have felt her in my blood ever since I was born and here she is now leaving a trace of perfume on my lips. She wipes dunes of fatigue from my forehead, and every time she visits, she sprinkles rosewater here in the folds of the prison, and on the threshold of my heart.

I entered my cell still holding onto Leila's insistence that I document the experience. I took out a sheaf of blank paper and a pencil and began to produce a draft on the subject. I started with an attempt at a history of the Left in our country. I then moved to some of the justifications for its existence and its ideological underpinning and structure, finally arriving at observations about its organizational makeup.

But why did our case encompass all these dimensions, and how did it manage to stretch from the realm of history into a surprisingly human reality? Can the specific conditions of the current reality during which the arrests took place somehow skip over all this apparent intransigence in the attitudes of the authorities toward issues that are considered legitimate human rights by the standards of international humanitarian law and the provisions of the country's constitution—i.e., freedom of belief, thought and organization? Why did the public prosecutor insist on charging us with conspiracy and attempting to overthrow the regime, all the while knowing that this stage could only be accomplished after the completion of two previous stages—also contained in the charges against us—which included spreading Marxist thought inside secret associations and attempting to form a political party that aimed to spread these ideas among different classes of people? But the charge of forming secret associations was just a misdemeanor punishable by no more than five years according to the legislator. It was a charge that we confessed to at all stages of the investigation, but the public prosecutor insisted on linking the charge of encouraging the strike to the charge of threatening state security. It was an issue that essentially aimed to create the appropriate climate to level harsh charges that did not line up with the nature of our movements. Twisting the facts in order to fit the rigid and existing legal texts has always been done this way. When I began to scrape away at the experience in all its dimensions, I did not intend to make it seem as if it had ended, or that it was like an empty bank account. I just felt the mistakes pressing down on my chest and I had to monitor them as such. We needed to confess, to grab a bit of boldness, in order to mourn this body that was no longer a clear statement to those coming from lighter industries or lines of work, to say that this moment was nothing more than a coffin where we spent these oppressive years. Imprisonment is, at the end of the day, imprisonment of the body. We were not obligated to demonstrate our steadfastness so our totems could become firmly established for those on the outside. We were in dire need of support that knew of our defeat, our split, and our fragmentation here in prison. To admit that prison was a double and slow deformation that destroys us, that erodes us. It depletes the soul and turns it into a desert where even mirages don't exist. Those who say that we are in the country's prison while they are in a country that is like a prison, too, are just talking nonstop nonsense. They have no voice. Nothing but prison is like prison. Only prison can be compared to prison. There's nothing else like it.

In fact, even when we push the dream halfway down the road and say that one day we'll get out of here, until we get out one day, could there possibly be a ritual capable of freeing us from the spiritual and physical consequences of prison that shows on our faces and courses through our veins? Prison is a place that each part of the body might come out of with nothing to hold them together.

7

I SAT IN THE PRISON yard. I stretched out my limbs—all my cramped limbs—in order to loosen up a little in the sun. I watched Moha as he paced. I gazed at him until I felt dizzy, then nauseous, so I closed my eyes to avoid him and wondered why Moha didn't get dizzy as he walked around in the same spot every day.

In the beginning, he would sit on the ground, put his face in his hands, and refuse to talk to us. After that he began to sit with his back to us, staring at the wall, his eyes overflowing with anger. Then he would start to cry. This is how he was now, talking to himself and no one else. He made wild sounds after which he would calm down and start to walk around in tight circles in the yard.

Moha tried to commit suicide twice, but the comrades' vigilance stood between him and death. The first time he came back from the hospital, he didn't utter a word. We talked to him, brought him food, took his clothes to be cleaned. As for the second time, after the comrades had helped him, as soon as he saw us walking toward him, he gathered up all his strength and started to back away from us. He pressed himself up against the wall and began to scream in our faces,

"What did I do with this hand? Tell me, what did I do?!"

"You slit it"

"What hand is this?"

"The left."

"Oh God. Dear Lord! I want to rip this 'left' from my veins and die, understand? From today on, no one gets anywhere near me. No one saves me!"

Moha screamed himself hoarse, spit flying out of his mouth.

We left him alone, each one of us dragging a heavy sadness. Wasn't it enough for Moha to transplant his pains into us? His words interrogated us from inside. Indeed, from vein to vein. This Moha was like someone who has been stabbed nearly to death, but who still possessed just enough life to question his tribe about the dagger they plunged in his back. His voice was like a whip cracking down on all our veins. Moha, who sprouted up with the green grass and wheat and wild thyme, who overflowed with sunshine, was the one most affected by the degradation we experienced here inside these prison walls. Moha, the only farmer among us, covered with the earth's greenery and wrapped in sunbeams, could not bear all this loss. Prison is continuous loss, and Moha did not know how to read or write, nor did he have a woman. Nothing could stand in for the smell of the village. Moha was taken from the curved sickle to certain drought, thrown straight from his village into prison. Placed between two, and only two extremes—being killed and destroying the soul, or playing a game of hide-and-seek where the player discovers that, in the end, he has gone blind.

Moha was lucky he was arrested just two days before the beginning of our trial, which meant he was spared the torture rituals. All he had to do was stick his thumb into the ink and press it onto the file folder that contained the list of charges. He thought that was it and then he would go back to his village after that. The only understandable and well-defined question he considered was whether he knew Ahmed Choufan, something he never denied. So, he joined us right away for the trial that would harvest not crops or wheat, but rather twenty years in prison, far from harvesting fields.

Throughout the court proceedings, Moha seemed dazed by the process and did not find it easy to swallow that he was with us in the context of an experience he had not confessed having close ties to. But how did Moha join the secret organization? Moha insisted on performing his prayers on time. That caused some of the comrades to make fun of him, and the gulf between him and us was wide from the start. They winked at one another while he used a small smooth stone one of the guards gave him to ritually wash himself before prayer. Everyone teased Ahmed Choufan, who came from the same village as Moha, saying to him,

"Say 'hi' to comrade Hadj Moha for us."

Moha didn't understand much of what we said or how we acted, but, as he put it one day, he felt suffocated when he was with us, and he provoked much discussion one evening when he laughed and said,

"Why do you speak like religious jurists? I don't understand you. You're like that family that starts to argue about who'll ride in the front seat of the car and who'll ride next to the windows in the back seat when they go buy a car, only for the father to tell them, 'Everyone out! I'll drive by myself,' and locks all the doors of the car he had never bought in the first place, and never would."

Moha cackled in our faces. We stood there staring, gazing at one another, recalling the rattle of his words. Were these words bullets? They were when Moha, whom we thought was deaf and dumb, uttered them. Moha didn't talk much. In fact, he barely spoke at all. I decided to throw caution to the wind and find out how this green peasant came to join our organization, how he became convinced of our political and ideological plan. We still believed that we would go to any length to achieve these plans. Moha surprised me with a question in response to my own question.

"What do you mean by 'organization'?"

"How did you come join *us*, here?"

I pointed to the rest of the comrades who were absorbed in group discussions.

"Why are you all called 'the organization'? You're Mouline. That's your name!"

"How did you come to know us?" And I pointed again to the rest of the comrades.

Moha assured me that he only joined up with us here in prison, and that he didn't know what I meant by many of the words I was using. At first, I thought he was being cagey or that he was just maintaining his silence on the matter, so I tried to reassure him. Then he went back and swore to God, religion, and his village that he loved so much that he didn't know any of us, and that he had never left his village before.

"You never left or travelled anywhere?"

"Just from one Monday to the next."

"The day of the cell meetings?"

"No, that's market day. What cell are you talking about? Do you mean beehive cells? We don't keep bees, and we don't make honey. Monday is market day. I'd ride my donkey, loaded up with whatever wheat and oil I was going to sell. Then, with that money, I'd buy what we needed and go back home. That's all the travelling I'd do."

"So, what's your relationship to Ahmed Choufan?"

"We come from the same village. Ah, that village . . ."

As soon as he said the name of his village, he went back to talking about its fields, its trees, the good people there . . .

Ahmed was Moha's friend. They started school together at the religious *kuttab* when they were seven years old. Moha ran away from the *kuttab* after two weeks to devote himself exclusively to caring for sheep, whereas Ahmed continued his studies, then travelled to the city. "But we remained friends. Brothers, even." That's how Moha said it, hardly putting it all together.

Of course, Ahmed told him about the city and the university. And he told him that we would soon take control of the government. That made Moha happy because Ahmed would become a governor and would no doubt turn to him. That's what he promised. He would tell him about all sorts of things in the city and ask what he thought about them, but Moha would just agree because "Ahmed was the educated one." Moha felt a special pride when he was asked for his advice and opinion on everything.

"I considered him a dear friend and would always tell him that you all were right, and he'd write down all of my 'yesses' in a little notebook."

I put my head in my hands. I felt the heat creep through my body and become concentrated in a spasm in my neck, which made me hear a buzzing sound in my temple.

Oh god, that's how the workers and peasants are brought into the party. That's how they join us. That's how you, Ahmed, netted a friend the size of earth's purity and wild thyme, that's how. I apologized to Moha (or maybe I didn't) and got up to go to the tap. I plunged my head under the stream of water, then took a long drink. I went back to a nearby spot, or was it far off? To the corner over there. I laid down flat on my belly. This Ahmed Choufan was mere proof of the sort of relationship that is established between someone and a peasant who thinks that someone is a party organizer. This was enough to embroil Moha in a game of obfuscation like in the Qur'anic story of the golden calf where the Israelites ask *what may it be . . . and what color may it be?*

My relationship with the leadership of our organization was not very close, but it wasn't too bad. I was a member of the Central Committee. Despite that, there was a tangible gulf between myself and many of these elements, with the exception of those who had been with me in the party before. Before washing our hands of it and joining the organization, we were members of the party's youth sector, only to find ourselves holding high level responsibilities in the new organization. Many of the members protested the rigidity of the party and called for the need to expand the field to allow new blood to flow through its structure, especially at the leadership levels.

I now viewed the experience from the present through eyes obscured by the blackness of this space. It was apparent to me that leaving the party was, in one respect, no more than a reaction. Was such a radical proposal a proposal in and of itself? Or was it necessary to rush forward only to set itself apart from where things currently stood? What sometimes confirmed the soundness of part of what I was now saying was that some of the leadership elements in here were starting to return—from prison back to the party— where they presented a self-criticism from here, from the prison. And after six months they were pardoned, their forgiveness checks cashed. Verily, the party is all-forgiving, all-merciful. Did we have to waste all this time just to go back one day to where we were before we started? I wasn't worked up or against the form of their assessment or what resulted in them returning to the party. Not at all. I was very angry now, just to protect myself. The anger had to take possession of me, otherwise it would finish me off to the point where I would convince myself that the movement had been nothing more than an initiative of reckless youth; a facilitator that wanted to sow revolution and ignite it in the hills and mountains, according to how the parties saw us. We were no more than a handful of troublemakers scheming with foreigners to overthrow the regime, according to the judgements passed down on us.

More than ever, I felt a need to protect myself from wear and tear. The project of documenting the experience was a sure-fire attempt to do so. Therefore, I dove right in. It is midnight and the sound of the ocean's waves reaches me, cleaving the darkness. It does not lessen my gloominess, but rather, increases it even more. This ocean, which I never saw as either male or female . . . here it is now coming to me to drink from my hand, approaching me. But the ocean is here. A woman slipping away like water from the palm of my hand.

The ocean is a woman when the woman is not here within reach. Thus, when night falls, Leila's specter rises up into my waiting sky. I wear its bright, pure garment. I gather up the scattered questions. I throw them there, far away, to where I can't reach. I remove their tumors from my heart. The paths might be long and Leila might not be able to tolerate the pain to the end.

I asked some questions and convinced myself only of the essence of the question. I got tired of wandering around the cellars of memory gathering up my experiences sealed with red wax—my school notebook, my first love, the smell of my mother's breast, my first kiss with Leila—as if I, after all of that resistance, were drinking it from the edges of knives, the tumult of years, the fever of time, the youthful freshness of my first surprise, my nom de guerre, my cup of coffee, my chair in the sun, familiar faces from my neighborhood, the sound of frogs croaking in the house's well.

I was still staring at my cell's ceiling, peeling the skin back from my memories, killing time, when one of dawn's threads slipped in from the cords of the night. I pulled the blanket over my face. I sank my head into my pillow to try to get back to sleep. I felt my bones coming apart. My body was trembling. My hands and feet were cold. I pulled my legs up to my chest and formed myself into a ball. This was how I had preferred to sleep ever since I was a child. Mama would stay up late to pull my knees away from my chest and rearrange the blanket over me. She would always tell me that sleeping all balled up like this would hinder my spine's flexibility and delay my growth spurt. So often I would try to stretch out straight before falling asleep, only to return to my balled-up position during the night. One night, I remember well. I thought she was heading to the toilet, but Mama took her time getting back to where she normally slept. I got up to look for her. I was eight years old. I heard muffled sounds in my father's room. I looked in through the crack in the door. I stared and I stared, and I saw her there on the same bed as my father! The room was small, with only enough space for one bed, but it was big enough for two. What was Mama doing next to my father? I burst into tears which made my father's whole body tense up in fear, and she burned with an embarrassment she couldn't hide from me for a long time. I didn't know that my coming into this world required bodies clinging together like that. I understood that this clinging and her having snuck away from me in the middle of the night to my father had happened many times before despite my snoring which hadn't allowed me to really sense it at all. That's how they sneak us into this world. They steal a moment at night when we're not watching to do what they need to do. They do this, without ever telling us that it's natural.

It is 11 a.m. and I am still collapsed in my bed with my eyes open. Were all these memories necessary? I got up out of bed completely exhausted. My head felt heavy, a mountain of stone. I grabbed the teapot, filled it with two cups of water, and lit the small burner. The water boiled and I pulled out a plastic bag of louiza, lemon verbena. I washed a few leaves and added them to the water in the pot. A glass of louiza used to be enough to bring me maximum relaxation, given my years-long addiction to this herb. Now that I have replaced it with green tea and headache pills, though, it could no longer bring on the relaxation it once did. My eyes hadn't closed all night. I was exhausted all day. I went back to bed and didn't get up until hunger began to gnaw away at my insides.

8

PRISON DAYS ARE IDENTICAL TO one another. They have no color other than black, but some days are more grueling than others. They cover the heart with cords of sadness and rust, casting clouds over the eyes. People rust behind bars. But I feel the spread of prison's cancer through my body most when communications between Leila and me are cut off. The connection between two people—one inside the prison and the other on the outside—does not always operate according to the logic of sympathy or the special circumstances of the situation. Rather, it might begin with sympathy and the delicate sense of our situation and our psyches. But as soon as the relationship deepens and becomes more clearly inscribed, the situation starts to change. An argument or a quarrel might sometimes develop into a total break.

Leila's absence is a prayer that tears me down, a stone cast at my heart. I approach my body and don't recognize it. I have come to resemble a smashed glass. How can I bounce back from pain to pain, after having been so torn apart? She is my strength, but enough pain upon pain. I return to my books and my poetry collections, and whenever my eye sinks into the lines, Leila rises from them. The poems grab ahold of me, and as fast as they destroy me, I find her taking possession of the whole alphabet, so how could I know which narcissistic doubts life had cast into the siege of death that has burned me up?!

So, Leila was gone. The sadness closed in, attaching its face to mine like a napkin sticks to the pages of a notebook. Outside the prison, it might happen that you fight with your girlfriend or that she fights with you, and when you feel the emptiness fill your heart, the decision to make your way to her grabs ahold of you. You throw yourself onto the next bus or train, even. You wait for an hour, or maybe four hours. It seems a long way to travel, even if it is just a mile from the nose on your face that you bury in the newspaper. And right after the headlines, small details weave a lifetime of your love. The train launches you back to the first time you met, and you rush to her as you say to yourself that she is the lock, she is the key. You knock on her door and embrace her, only to melt in her arms.

A woman might get angry at you, driving you to the point of misery, but when you hug her, when you put your arms around her waist, place your hands gently on her neck, and kiss her, you melt like butter in her arms.

But it happens that our girlfriends get mad, and there isn't enough time to make up with them in this place where time pursues us with the ending's stick. She arrives at the doorstep and might not turn around, and I am here, fixed in place in spite of myself, dripping sadness and grief. *She* takes a step there, through the prison gate, while *I* stand here, forsaken, no star reaching me and no imagined hug to provide me with shelter for the night. Thus, my loneliness multiplies. I feel like I'm fading away. I open my throat wide and shout out her name, but there's no one to answer save for an echo that reverberates between the bars and walls. The name "Leila" remains stuck in my throat and I am at a loss as to whether I should push it out or stuff it back inside. That's how we are here, when we can't grab onto something from the outside. I divide my throat and my entire body between outside and inside and, like all my comrades, imagine that I'm knocking on the door of my body and going in and out whenever I please. But who will pour the glow into my body when Leila isn't there? Who will reinvigorate the song, even with paleness? Leila is my rhythm and I am an orphan who has gotten lost in unreachable alleys. Leila is not there, so inevitably everything is orphaned. We are those posted in two separate places—my body here, my heart there—and when I try to move toward her, I cannot. This is how this country is. Whenever I call out, it gives me prisons. This is how this country is. Hajjaj bin Yusuf, the famous Umayyad governor, is the one who legalized its first and second to last history, saying, "He who utters a word we imprison or kill, and he who remains silent dies of grief."

That's how I am now. Leila is not here and there's no one to pour the blazing glow into my body, nor is there anyone to shove the larvae out from inside my tired head. Leila is not here and there's no one to rouse my dreams or gather up my sobs. That's how it is when we fight. While I am in prison I can't make up with Leila or even apologize. All I have is paper, so I can fill the pages. I safeguard my longings and torment, which deprives me of sleep. Dawn sends some of its threads and we realize that our only solace is in words. Cold sweat covers my body. We sit on the ground, repeating to ourselves: Prison is agony and sadness and grief. Prison is barren. Sterile. A wasteland.

Once, after visiting her husband here in prison, Rabia carried news of my deteriorating health to Leila and she came to me right away the following day. I couldn't believe it when I was called to the visit. Salah told me it was Leila. I went like a child crawling toward the breast. I didn't know whether I should go out in my pajamas or change my clothes. The important thing was that there was no time to waste. Leila was here, filling me up before I even saw her. I had felt tired for two weeks, coughing nonstop. I had become the prisoner who was suffering the most from runny noses. My immune system had weakened considerably since my imprisonment, which I felt twice as much when fall and then winter came calling. I had no desire to go to the hospital. How would I feel if I went to the hospital and did not find Leila waiting for me? Before, going there was a relief, a dream that would stand against my deterioration. We would pull up to the hospital door. We would get out of the Land Rover. We would turn right and left. We would feel a cool breeze. We would turn toward the people there; all those who had seemed so tired to us before. Clones, piled up with wrinkles of sweat and years. They looked different now. Changed. Looking like people who filled their lungs with air when they pleased. People who seemed as cheerful as could be compared to us. The guards urged us to walk faster.

"C'mon, hurry up now. Enough chitchat!"

We would leave the guard's words behind us at the door and enter the hospital to embrace the women who awaited us there. Even though the hospital was a broken space, a space for sickness, our rendezvous with women made it a warm place where we recited verses, proclamations of love, and enjoyed touches and passion.

For the fifteen days we were arguing, I had no desire to go to the hospital. Without Leila there, it would feel like an agony no less than the agony of prison.

I decided not to tell Leila yet about my anxieties. My distress was enough for her. Prison is one heavy burden after another. I don't remember how I broached a subject I felt I understood better than anyone else. I don't know how that happened, but she seemed fresh to me that day, and I asked her if she was as much of a mystic with me as I was with her.

I felt her tremble—her hands, her lips—before speaking.

"I'm not Rabia al-'Adawiyya and I don't want you to be al-Hallaj. You ask me while you're in here. You don't have the freedom to choose when I come to you here, whereas I possess *all* the freedom to choose."

I didn't say a word, but I felt the awfulness of where I had put myself. From Leila's silence, and the way her eyes drooped toward the ground, I understood her annoyance, how sharp her anger was. I took her hand and placed it in mine, but she

72

immediately pulled it away and got up. The day before yesterday, the allotted visiting time was not enough for us. We filled the time telling stories, expressing our love for one another. The guard, Allal, kept putting off alerting us to the time until the rest of the comrades had finished up in the corridor and Leila was the last visitor there. This time, we still had an hour and fifteen minutes before the end of the visit and Leila wanted to leave. She said goodbye and left. I felt like she had left for real. And so, it was undone like a hair holding two ribs together. And here she was coming back. After today, I'll stop digging for things that are buried away, hidden. Her fragrance was enough for me. She appeared and looked at me. Leila satisfies me. She fulfills me. I went out to her. She seemed radiant, shimmering. She raised her hand to greet me as she asked about my health. I embraced her. I hugged her. I passed my lips all over her face, along the sides of her neck. She let out a laugh as she slipped away. We sat and it was as if it was our first time meeting as we broached the topic of our love for one another. Whenever a bit of silence hung in the air between us, I tried to fill it quickly so Leila wouldn't be upset by what we had been arguing about again. When you're a prisoner, you just ask for a basket; it doesn't need to have grapes in it. That's what Ahmed Choufan would always say, but Leila was grapes for the soul and orange for the body. Grapes that have matured and that give off their alcoholic sweetness. All of a sudden, we found ourselves moving to a discussion about the last conference. I asked her all about it, and she zig-zagged, seemingly aimlessly, to comment on the president's reelection, and she wondered if Badia, Brahim's ex-wife, could be compelled to run for the same position. No matter what energies and potentials she might have shown, had she given herself and her body this "right?" Believe me, had she lived a normal relationship, when she promoted her candidacy for the same position, the society of militants would have said, "No. No, not possible. She's a whore!"

"But Si Brahim? He had the right to dance, pinch, and recite pacts. I don't know why you're so insistent on dredging up the memory of polygamy even when you find love and wrap yourselves in ideals," said Leila.

"We're the product of a historical condition."

"And do *we* just emerge out of thin air?" she asked sarcastically.

"I don't think so, but this situation, as it stretches and expands, has come to lay down in front of us as if it were something normal, following its natural course. Every man enters into a relationship with a woman. He falls in love with her. He marries her. But, although he places marriage in the center, that doesn't prevent him from forming peripheral relationships. Had it not been for this implicit agreement, the institution of marriage might not have lasted this long . . . "

"So, everything that happens is natural, then. Is it possible, according to this logic, that *we* have these relationships that are peripheral to a central one? A relationship with the husband and relationships with . . . "

"That wouldn't be acceptable because it's framed within a historical context."

Leila burst out laughing as she waved her hands in front of my face, confirming that we were operating according to nothing more than a presumptuous drumbeat that would not humble itself and would never stop searching for the awaited mehdi, or guide, from among us, without us writing in the margins that this mehdi might bear the face of a woman.

I laughed approvingly at what Leila said and hugged her. I confirmed that in her presence, I acknowledge that she is my prophet and my mehdi who comes and puts an end to my waiting.

Leila as she is now, the one who takes great pains to visit me, is different from the Leila I first knew. It wasn't joy that brought us together, perhaps because our relationship did not become entirely clear to me until after I was in prison;

perhaps because, after all this loss we have lived through, we have become aware of all these things we weren't aware of before when we held them in our grasp.

Before I was in prison, whenever Leila visited, silence would envelop me. I would pass my eyes over her face and the sides of her neck as if pushing prayer beads one after the other as I recited verses of silence in her presence.

Leila fills me up. The visit ended and I rushed back to my cell. I had finished knitting a wool scarf. I hurried back out to her. I wrapped it around her neck. It was orange and Leila shimmered in it. I grabbed her. I embraced her. I pinched her, or rather, I squeezed her. We kissed and she left. I stood where I was until she disappeared from view. The gate closed and I headed back to the prison garden. I hadn't looked at my seedlings for fifteen days. I hadn't watered them. I hadn't asked about them. I sat down near the marigolds. I dangled my feet in the bushes and filled a small bucket of water. I watered some louiza, or verbena, as Salah calls it, and continued to gaze at the marigolds. Marigolds possess the unique ability to burst forth suddenly, and just as suddenly slip away and hide. They will appear at the peak of brilliance, petals in full bloom, then all of a sudden, without any prior warning, they'll start to sag. They wilt at the neck, stamens shrinking. That's how marigolds sum this place up. You imagine them in their seventh stage of sleep. You might be away from them for some time and when you go back, when you walk by them, they'll surprise you as they awaken, proudly raising their heads.

Salah noted that I was like a marigold in full bloom. One whose head had just started to nod. He walked over to me. We sat together on the ledge, our legs against the wall.

"Just yesterday you were sitting here in the corner of sadness, in the middle of the night. Today, here you are joyfully peeling the wrinkles off marigolds."

I laughed and gave Salah's palm a slap.

"How can we live without women?"

"And coffee, and wine, and cigarettes, and . . ."

Salah laughed as he made his list of necessities before cutting the sarcasm and asking in all seriousness,

"Who said she came from a crooked rib bone? I swear, if they just went back a bit in history, Adam would admit that the apple was nothing more than a flimsy insult. Had Eve not been there in the garden, Adam would have tendered his resignation before the expulsion decree had been issued for him."

"She's not from a crooked rib bone, and she isn't always a snake. Just as not every woman can tempt man with a forbidden apple, not every man can offer a gesture to the lord."

This Salah—despite our detention, despite the sadness that cast its shadow over our faces—more than any of us, remained the embodiment of extended childhood, undefeated by torture or the darkness of prison. Salah's laugh was pure; you didn't feel that it came with any effort, nor did you sense any dust had settled on it. He was never overly amazed. Every new thing that happened to him amazed him. Salah received the same sentence I did. His girlfriend, Souad, here in the women's ward in Gharbia, was sentenced to four years. After a year of denied requests to the administration that they be allowed to visit one another, they decided to get married. The administration based its refusal to let them see one another on the fact that we lived in a conservative society, and that our country does not recognize a free relationship between an unmarried couple. But if there were a legal bond between them, things would be much easier. So, Salah and Souad decided to get married since getting together otherwise was proving to be so difficult. It didn't require any more than presenting the request to the prison administration along with specific documents (copies of their birth certificates and pictures of their ID cards). However, it took four months for the approval to arrive, after which the idea had lost much of the luster it had possessed when it was first presented. No doubt the matter reached the highest levels of the country from the

Ministries of Justice, Interior, Exterior, and so on. We constantly ribbed Salah about it:

"You'll transform the prison into a wedding hall. Would all these cadres and organizations know about your marriage if you weren't here in the 'house of safe and sound?'"

"The important thing is for you to be fully prepared and ready to go. Whoever receives word of it should consider themselves invited to the celebration."

"Say, who will sit to your left. I mean, who will be your best man, your 'minister?'"

"The Minister of the Interior, of course. I'll seat him to my left, if only this one time."

"No, we want him to stand for it. If he's going to sit, forget about it. Just picture it. The Minister of the Interior sitting to your left, but he stands there on the far right. No. It would be better if you picked your best man from among us, only us."

The prison administration didn't give us too much time when they informed Salah in the morning that his marriage to Souad would take place at around 3:30 that afternoon. Despite the short notice, we decorated the yard by dragging in all the beds and covers, and picking a bunch of marigolds that were, that day, at the peak of their radiance. We laid them as a garland in the center of the yard and arrayed them all around its edges as well. We filled small plastic buckets with water and threw leaves into them to float on the surface. We wanted the entire space to appear green.

Salah, whom we had taken in spite of himself to the prison bath, came out into the yard and was taken aback. Four of us comrades linked hands to form a divan and we sat him on it. We had him wear the white jilbab and babouche slippers the families had brought two weeks after the marriage request had been put to the prison administration. Since then, we had hidden the clothes from Salah until we brought them out to him that day and he was overwhelmed, like a poet rendered speechless by heated applause. We were so happy for Salah, and imagined that the atmosphere in the women's ward was even more festive. No doubt, the women comrades' preparations would be no less animated than ours. It was 3 p.m. We seated Salah on a divan with a white cover and four pillows on it strewn with marigolds. Just fifteen minutes before the notary was to come in to perform the ceremony and Souad was to be brought in, the guard, Allal, came to summon Salah to the warden's office. We asked him what was going on and he informed us that the two notaries had arrived and that things would happen in the administrative building, in the warden's office. No sooner had Allal finished speaking did we explode in protest. It was an insult aimed to strike us at our core. We shouted and voiced our disapproval. We were furious. The rest of the guards hurried in, joined by the Commander. We were prepared not only to shout to the ends of the earth, but for a full rebellion; blows; injury; even for casualties to fall on both our side and the administration's! The guards took a step back while the Commander slinked away, thinking he could get away with it. He came back after a little while to tell us that he was not going to implement any more recommendations from the higher-ups, and that he had just contacted them to inform them of our protests demanding that the marriage be done in the yard with all of us present. But they told him to wait as well so that *they* could ask permission from other, even *higher* higher-ups.

The two notaries continued to wait in the Commander's office, and Souad waited in the women's ward. We remained standing, insisting that our voices be heard.

It was a quarter to five when the Commander's phone rang, and he received the order that we celebrate Salah and Souad as we wished. Allal rushed in to tell us, then went back to escort the Commander and the two notaries, then Souad. We couldn't have been happier, and we hugged Salah as we led him to the threshold of the main door through which Souad would enter. She appeared fresh as a carnation wearing a white shirt and flipflops. We watched her approach as

Salah walked forward to take her by the hand. She was not surrounded by comrades, though. Rather, she was accompanied by two guards who looked out of place next to her. We knew that this was according to orders. At first, we were excited to see the female comrades who had experienced pain and shared such an experience with us, despite the particulars of their situation. Salah held out his hands to receive Souad and they threw themselves into one another's arms. Souad looked beautiful. She walked toward us and we rushed over to surround her. We longed to see our female comrades who had shared the bitterness of imprisonment with us. They were deserving of a kiss on the forehead.

"Kiss Souad on the forehead. Souad is our saint today, Salah."

"No, Souad is my saint. Just mine."

"Look at how many Cains and Abels surround you."

"That was in the pre-stone age. We're in the age of democracy, now. There's a choice between Cain, meaning me, or all of you Abels . . ."

Right on, Salah! This age of democracy is what marries you off in prison. I felt that talking was too painful, so we all raised our voices in song.

Abid, Jalil, and Anas took care of serving the tea and drinks that we bribed Allal to bring us, as well as distributing the sweets that had gotten a bit cold because they had been sitting out for so long. But regardless. And the wine. It was the first time we had had it in prison, brought in by some friends. We had hidden some of it just for this day. We tried as much as we could to reclaim the atmosphere. As for Salah and Souad, they sat facing one another, their hands intertwined. There were still too few pillows, so they sat right on the ground. Because the situation required eyewitnesses, and because there were more than enough with all of us in attendance, the two notaries began to marry the couple with their traditional question to Souad.

"Do you accept the groom, Salah Ribaoui, to be your husband?"

We burst out laughing at the question. It probably would not have seemed so silly to us had we not been in prison.

Souad had gathered her hair up and pinned it into a bun. Her hairstyle, which went with her round, brown face, made her neck appear as long as a road with no end. We asked Salah to undo the hairpins like the Bedouins do; we very much needed to embrace our essence. The two notaries finished reciting the Fatiha prayer for a second time. We poured them some tea and they left while we urged Salah and Souad to dance for us as we sang. They stood up and danced to the sound of us beating on plates and buckets and singing our wild songs. Temporary pleasures. Best of all was that we discovered how powerful a voice Boujmaâ had when he sang popular songs we didn't dare sing (they used to call songs with bad words "popular songs"). Boujmaâ regaled us with his singing that went on and on until the Commander cleared his throat as he stepped forward to ask that we end the marriage rituals. It was 6.30. That's how he said it as he turned his eyes to his wristwatch.

We looked up. We stared at him as if we didn't understand. The Commander snapped a second time, and then a third for us to wake up to the fact that Souad had to go back to the women's ward. The order fell on us like a whip soaked in salt. We asked the warden for an explanation, and he said that the marriage contract had only been completed to make it easier for them to be able to visit one another, not for Souad to take up permanent residence here. If that were the case, we would end up transforming the prison into a hotel, then into a children's daycare!!

"And the consummation?"

The Commander let out a laugh unlike any we had heard before.

"There'll be no 'going in' until you're all let out!"

Souad began to drag her feet toward the door at the end of the yard that led to another steel door to the women's prison yard which, in turn, led to their ward. That's how Souad described their space to us. We all walked her to the door. She gave Salah a long hug. Her tears glistened in her eyes, ready to fall onto her radiant face. All of us were dripping sadness. We dragged ourselves back, gripping Salah's shoulder, his hands. The door closed in our faces and Souad disappeared from view; Souad, who had granted us a bit of deferred joy that was now broken in the furthest reaches of our hearts. How would Salah sleep on his wedding night? Thus we went back to our ward, chewing on our pain . . . lumps in our throats. Salah had a crushed look in his eyes. In an attempt to ease his agony, all of our agony, I said to him,

"Tonight, you'll produce poetry. Don't let this night pass without poetry."

We entered our cells and collapsed in a heap, arranging a memory that burned for a long time. We had thought that, following the wedding, the relationship between us and the female comrades would be facilitated through Souad who would visit Salah whenever she wanted. However, prison is prison, no matter how bright it might seem on its face. Like an old shoe whose cracks don't disappear just by having it shined. For the two years that remained of Souad's sentence, you could count on one hand the number of times Salah was able to see her. The administration stood firm on not allowing additional visits or extending their length, justifying themselves by claiming that this marriage was only executed with the goal of easing communication between us and the female comrades so that we could coordinate and encourage them to go on strike.

For the duration of the female comrades' detention, issued statements were few, rare in fact. Their first statement had to do with the first anniversary of Samad Mehdaoui's martyrdom. We understood their situation, especially the psychological aspect of it vis-à-vis their relationships with their

families. Naturally, their suffering on this level was complicated. Few of the female comrades' families understood that
they were in a political prison, or that they were there on
account of their opinions.

The idea of women serving time in prison fell outside
of social and familial norms, and that was enough of a justification for their families to wash their hands of them. We
knew the pressures this caused and the double suffering that
weighed down heavily on them. But however much we might
have tried, we could not grasp the specifics of their situation.
Therefore, we looked forward to receiving news about all
the female comrades when we met with Souad. But it was a
broken dream and the female comrades' situation remained
scattered, with no one to put it back together. In secret and
in public, we would speak about their unparalleled ability to
tolerate adversity that they displayed while they were in secret
detention. But who wrapped up such beautiful bright lights so
tightly and threw them in here, into this country's prison cells?
Who will dust these flowers off?

Most of the female comrades, including Souad, got out of
prison after four years. We called out to them from the yard.
Just the fact that they were getting out was enough to rebuild
many of the bridges between them and their families. When
Souad got out, she devoted herself to visiting Salah. Other
female comrades devoted themselves to visiting us as well,
which livened up the atmosphere somewhat, and the dossier
of romantic relationships began to open, then fill up. To this
day, I don't know how relationships were born between this
comrade and that woman, and not between him and someone
else. Such deep and intimate things as relationships between
people, especially romantic ones, are impossible to grasp.

I still remember perfectly Salah coming to my cell one
evening after the end of one of Souad's visits.

"Listen Mouline, Souad and I have decided to have a
child this year."

I looked closely at him. Nowhere was there any sign of sarcasm or joking around. Salah was as serious as can be.

"And how's that going to happen? You're well aware of the situation."

"We'll arrange everything, we . . . "

"Who do you mean?"

"Me, you, Souad, Abid, his uncle."

"Wait, slow down. I don't get it. What do Abid and I have to do with your decision. And who's his uncle?"

"You're the Executive Committee. No, sorry, you're the Organizational Committee . . . "

"Meaning?"

"You remember Ouahab? Abid's uncle? The soldier who was guarding us when we were recovering after the hunger strike?"

To be honest, I had practically forgotten about him. Ouahab went to great lengths to facilitate communication between us and our families. I remember the day he took it upon himself to convey a statement and distribute it widely to the newspapers with the utmost confidentiality. A patriotic man who carried all the characteristics of a resistance fighter, but with whom independence was stingy when it stripped him of his resistance fighter card and tossed him aside to become a soldier guarding children of the nation.

Salah clarified his plan for me. He would be stricken with a stomachache for a week during which time he would only go to the prison clinic. This would culminate in a severe attack, which would result in his transfer to the hospital where he would need to undergo tests that might take three days or more.

"What matters to me is just one night, and Souad will visit me that night. Of course, we'll arrange things with Ouahab through his nephew, Abid, who's here with us."

I listened to Salah as if I were listening to a cassette tape recording or a draft proposal for a story or novel project. He laid out the details.

"Where'd you come up with all this?"

"Pain works its way with poets, writers, and engineers too!"

Salah jumped up having decided. He asked me to go with him to talk with Abid so we could start making the arrangements that night. Salah, Abid, and I sat in my cell. Salah took out a piece of paper and a pen and began to plan out loud.

"Right now it's July 10th. Souad is menstruating. Her fertile phase will be in a week, so we'll arrange the meeting during this and that day . . . "

"You don't think one night is enough?"

Laughing, Abid added,

"So the stomachache needs to start the day after tomorrow, and we need to arrange everything with my uncle."

Ouahab did not object when he was informed of the plan through his sister, Abid's mother. He just needed to know that Salah and Souad were legally married. This was confirmed by Abid's mother so he agreed. We never found out how Uncle Ouahab was able to secure the night watch for himself the day he took Salah to the hospital.

Whenever the pain from the stomachache caused Salah to yell out, we would rush to his side. I hadn't imagined he could fake all that pain. The three of us avoided looking at one another so as not to burst out laughing. Rather, we rushed over to him so we would get there before any of the other comrades which might have exposed the ruse. Salah wouldn't stand up to any serious scrutiny of his condition from the comrades. They urged him to go straight to the hospital while he insisted the pain would pass after a visit to the prison doctor and some tranquilizers. The three of us—Abid, Salah, and I—had to keep the matter to ourselves.

The weekend arrived and Salah's stomachache culminated in an acute attack. Abid and I almost believed it. He was taken to the hospital where Uncle Ouahab, the nighttime soldier, received him from the daytime guard. Souad came to him there and it was a done deal.

Except that Salah didn't return to the prison right away because the tests showed that he was in urgent need of an appendectomy. We couldn't believe this news that Rabia brought us folded up in a letter from Souad.

The rest of the comrades took the matter in stride considering how acute Salah's stomachache had been the week before he went into the hospital. It was just Abid and I who had to stifle our laughter until we got to our cells and exploded in laughter.

"The pig got what he was looking for!"

Abid and I decided to visit the hospital. The administration filled out a form for eye exams after we asked if Allal could go with us. We pressed the issue because of the many bonds that had been forged between us. These bonds had begun with bribery, but they subsequently established themselves into something resembling friendship. We walked into Salah's room and the three of us burst out laughing.

"Brother, we wondered how you became such a master at faking the pain!"

Salah tried to hug us, but we prevented him from doing so as we leaned down to kiss him. IVs were still stuck into his right hand and his face looked a bit pale.

We asked for details about that night. Laughing, he told us everything and added,

"What's life without a child and a woman in it?"

"So quickly. Even before it arrives, when you say it, you put the child before Souad."

"And you, aren't you good at anything other than digging into my every word?"

Even after the tryst between Salah and Souad was done, they both feared she wouldn't get pregnant, but before Salah returned to the prison after about a month, the first piece of news Souad brought to us was of her pregnancy. It was a momentous day. We were so happy for him and the news spread slowly but surely until all the comrades knew. Once the details were revealed, some of the others might be encouraged to try the same thing, even though arranging the meeting with their wives did not necessarily guarantee a child. The issue of infertility was never raised, but psychological factors could not be entirely discounted. In any case, Souad's belly began to swell as we closely watched Salah wait for his child, counting each day of her pregnancy.

9

I WAITED FOR LEILA BUT she didn't come. I was confused. I didn't know why she didn't show up. She usually told me ahead of time that she wouldn't be there. Or she would send her apologies with one of the other visitors. Today, Leila didn't come, and neither did an apology. There was only a quarter of an hour left of visiting time and I was still waiting at the end of the corridor, looking out for her to appear at the prison gate. Visiting hours ended and she didn't show. As Rabia was saying goodbye to her husband, I asked her to call Leila and let me know the following day through Souad why she didn't show up. Souad would be visiting Salah. But Leila came the next day before Souad did. She looked broken, sad.

"What's up? Are you sick?"

"No, no. I'm fine."

"I was worried about you yesterday. I didn't know what happened."

"Si Ahmed came to my house and I couldn't leave him. He was hurt."

"What happened?"

"A fight broke out between two factions in the party, and it blew up yesterday during the Central Committee meeting."

"How did that come about? What happened exactly?"

"Right now, the details are foggy, but what's clear is that the police got involved to break up the fight and they had to arrest most of the members of the Central Committee."

"But the meeting was inside the headquarters. How is that possible? How'd the police get involved?"

"No. Rather members of the Executive Committee were inside the headquarters. The other faction was prevented from entering with the justification that it had been expelled from the party, and members of the Central Committee were bent on attending the meeting. That's how things came to blows and the police were called."

Even though we had left the party and had joined the secret organization, and despite the party having pretended not to acknowledge us, not even to come to our defense during the trial, I was upset and felt a pain pressing down on my heart about what had happened. We had started to ring in the second decade of our detention, and the party's positions had started to improve vis à vis its relationship with us whether it was publishing our creative projects and statements without deleting or cutting anything, or demanding our release through other rights associations and parallel organizations to it.

That day, Leila looked like a stronghold of sadness. I sensed her tears as they glistened in her eyes. But Leila was always like this. Even in the most emotionally charged situations, you'll find tears in her eyes, but they won't trickle down her face. Leila's silent crying baffles me. When she holds the tears back and they disappear, leaving her eyes moist, they are as intensely expressive as they are strongly indifferent. It's as if the tears have been stricken with fatigue.

I gazed into her eyes for a long time, and I don't know why, right then, I remembered the author, José Cela who compared the woman who doesn't cry to a spring that has run dry, or a bird that has stopped singing. Never in my life had I seen a woman as waterless as those described by Cela, but Christie, who came from Europe, destroyed all our notions of what western women were like. Ever since she had connected with Boujemaâ, she was like a spring that never dried up. A passionate woman, laser-focused. Our dossier was published in detail—included in Amnesty International reports—and based on that, she decided to shower us with letters, after which she settled on choosing to correspond with Boujemaâ. He was the one who would compel her to move to our country and work here, and she proceeded to make her way to Gharbia like any of this country's simple people. When our dossier was published, it included a report on our situations, along with our pictures, birthdates, and detention numbers. That's right. We had been transformed into numbers without names after ten years and counting. We felt the impact of having been transformed into numbers at first, and ruminating over this as the years went by had created a special familiarity between us and our numbers. It was a number rather than a name that we would look at on the back of an envelope. Once I asked Salah,

"Is it possible that we might, one day, forget our numbers?"

"Is it possible that we might, one day, remove our skin?" he responded.

Leila remained unfocused and sad for the entire visit. I tried to dress her wound with some words about the travails the party had known since the beginning, pointing out that all these contradictions that have always culminated in internal explosions at the party level would only serve its interests in the long term. This path didn't harm the party or erase it. Rather, it was its wealth, its inheritance. From the Shouri and Independence parties to the National Union and the Socialist Union parties, the fighting only worked to put down deeper roots now more than it worked to defeat it.

"But things here with us only grow bigger to then break apart."

I hardly noticed that Leila was making an effort to utter these words through deep sighs when I put my hand on her neck and played with some wisps of her hair. She drew closer and threw her head onto my shoulder, closing her eyes a bit.

Until now, I have been unable to figure out what Leila's effective position was concerning the party, what wing she was with. I didn't know at all. But I could be sure of one thing: Leila was as sad as she was trustworthy. She would search long and hard for a piece of information and when you get the chance to touch what you are seeking, she lets you pull the threads of interpretation from over here, and put them over there, as happened that year.

We were still in the party, members of the Youth Organization, when Leila had enrolled in the university and then with us, or so we thought. She was an object of interest to everyone, but it was at the student conference where her light was discovered, for the process of her attracting a regular ritual for all of the movement's components to begin. That's how she was: still as a leaf you fear might be blown away by a breeze, while at the same time, sharp as an arrow. Leila joined extremes to one another, but until now, I didn't understand the effective reasons for this and sometimes would reject putting any trust in her, as the comrades piled all those burdens on her. After they became the real beneficiaries of her movements, Leila continuously refused to join the organization. But never for a day did she keep the comrades from interacting with her as one of them. The reason she always gave was that the time hadn't come yet, and that joining the organization was a source of anxiety for her. But a bunch of issues had not become clear yet, and the comrades insisted on knowing what these issues were when Leila wasn't there. When she *was* there, the comrades remained silent. She insisted that it was personal and connected to her particular upbringing. I felt that Leila was acutely aware that the organization's pressure on her had increased, especially after failing to win her heart. And it had.

"If a woman isn't attached to some man in the party, they think about attaching her to the party itself."

The comrades bet a lot on me to attract Leila emotionally to the party organization, especially since her relationship to the comrades was neutral, if not cold, as compared to with me. I felt her to be in a constant state of high alert whenever the topic of the relationship was broached, but deep down, to my core, I was working with Leila who had slipped in and begun to burrow into all of my pores. She filled me up and I pushed back on my desire to devour her, afraid she would slip away from me forever. Even with all her boldness, Leila would not face the comrades and explain why she was putting off joining. The scene was clear, and Leila was an unfounded escape. Once I asked her about the women's organization and its place within the party. She gazed at me for a long time and shot a question back at me in response to my own.

"Does the party really have a women's organization? There's nothing but men and their wives in the party."

The way the comrades lured women into the organization did not appeal to Leila. I knew that well. Women came to the student yard, and even to the student associations, as flames. No one denied the comrades' primary act of incorporating them into the core of the movement. But as soon as the romantic connection—the flame—started to go out and the retreat to second class was complete (and this would happen quickly), the women were hidden inside the home. Was this the fault of these women, these comrades, or was it just how things were?

I felt that the process of women's development, when it was done by way of betting on a friend or a comrade or a lover, was rarely pushed to its limit, even within the necessary limits. That's how it was. When the risk that the relationship be invigorated by others, and not by reality, the self comes up short.

With the rumors against Leila piling up, those starting and spreading those scenarios could not imagine the psychological toll it was taking on her. In fact, that was not on their minds at all. However, if Leila could muster up the energy to restrain herself while she was being assaulted and disparaged by vicious tongues suspicious of her behavior, then what they threw at her, or even just grabbed at, would destroy her and erect barricades between us and her. I don't know why whenever a woman would run from them to higher ground, they would try to eject her by accusing her of being an agent of the police or of being a prostitute. Leila could not be controlled, so flushing her out was inevitable.

We did not see Leila among us anymore. She was present at the core of the sector's strategy, but she was absent from our orbit. That's why she was deemed suspect first in her behavior, then as something that sabotaged the movement. Leila was from the police. She was cast out on account of that accusation one morning and word of it was on everyone's tongue that day and every day after. It was broadcast far and wide. Leila finally put an end to the comedy by accepting Mohammed's marriage proposal.

Leila's existence still pervades me. I know this, as does Amina, despite her belief that Leila's marriage to Mohammed would pull me back together and that *we*, Amina and I, would begin our path together. But it was no use. Leila's presence fills me up, every one of my pores. Amina continued to visit me even with Leila's presence coursing through me, so Amina turned to Abbas and they got married.

I tried to staunch the flow of Leila through my veins after she married Mohammed, but as soon I heard her name, she would rise up and fill my whole body. I wanted to find a limited place for her inside me, but it was difficult. One thing I know, but don't quite understand, is how Leila was a presence that lived inside me. Now, I recall what was contrived against her and I remember her as she knocked on my apartment door. Hushed knocks. When I opened the door, her voice was choked. She greeted me with her head down. As soon as I saw her, I felt myself trembling all over. She sat down on the single sofa there, and I sat down in front of her.

"I know, Mouline, that I'm not a part of the organization, which means I don't have the right to inquire about some of its internal affairs. But please listen and tell me, who knows about the organizing members?"

"These are internal affairs. It's true that we consider you close, despite your refusal to join the organization, but trust me, I don't know the ones who are sympathetic to the organizers. The ones I know are in the youth organization and I could count them on one hand. You know that work in the party is done through two separate faces: a public face, and a secret internal face. This latter one is implemented through cells, and each cell consists of no more than five members."

"Of course, theoretically, that's what I know about the organizational level. And that's what I want to confirm now. But reality is something else entirely. Can you tell me which cell Hafez belongs to? How about Abbas? Lahcen? Reda?"

Leila's response hit me like ton of bricks as I mulled over her question.

"What happened exactly?"

"In the university courtyard, within earshot of many people, I met Latifa with some other students. They were chatting about the arrest campaigns and she was confirming that the issue didn't go beyond members who had recently joined the organization, along with those who, before, were members of the radical wing. Then she began to list the names I mentioned to you."

I tried to assume an air of indifference, even though I felt troubled by what she had fallen into. I agreed with Leila concerning everything she said, even her conclusions, which I am ashamed to express. What do you have to do with all of this, Mustafa? And what do I say if Leila finds out that you are the coordinator between this cell and others? Does all the steeliness of the organization become a trap that is prepared for the girl from the first light of a beautifully adorned morning until the last traces of daytime as she goes to sleep at night? What happened to you? I know Leila came to a similar conclusion, but her shy reluctance to stir all of that up will excuse me from getting involved. When I recall how bold she was when she stimulated our deepest concerns, I immediately recalled her childlike shyness in other things, and she replenishes me yet again.

Three days after she visited me at home, after I had calmed down a bit, I went to see Mustafa. He assured me he hadn't meant it, and told me about an impromptu meeting he had been forced to call because he was to travel that night to Tunis to meet the faqih who had been present at the general orientation of that strategy session. He had to communicate the planning details before travelling to Syria. Latifa was at home. Perhaps she had figured it out after the comrades left that evening.

We looked at the problem again from every angle, and I assured him that the carelessness originated from him, and from the comrades who had agreed to meet here at the house under these circumstances.

The party was going through a difficult historical juncture, determined mainly by the insistence of some nationalists that independence had forced them to lay down their arms, and that their response to this had been a fatal mistake that could only be remedied by assembling the rest of the nationalists in other countries and searching for a storage place that the Makhzen could not reach. The issue was presented at the leadership level favoring some, but not all, cells from the youth organization. Mustafa's cell was one of those concerned.

I struggled mightily for a way to ask the question, but Mustafa insisted it would not happen again. We shelved it, but I wasn't convinced.

Right after that, rumors began to ensnare Leila, moving between attacking her behavior and her positions. The important thing was that Leila had been placed in the yard's laboratory where she was being poked and prodded. Echoes of that reached her. Actually, a series of comrades' accounts about her had begun quite nastily behind her back, only reaching her indirectly. But the last rumor made her place a definitive distance between herself and the comrades of the recent past.

She continued to visit me, albeit very sporadically. We didn't talk a lot. I would have liked to have dug through that file a little bit, but it was hard on me, so I made do with her just being there. With all the topics we brought up together, I felt as if I were rearranging my memory according to what I had read. All of this was so as not to leave a void when I sat with her. When she got up and said goodbye, I decided that during the next visit, I would let *her* talk, and when she was done, the empty void would continue. I wanted it to remain a void. As long as there was a void, it would be filled by heartbeats, with one heart listening to the other.

During her second to last visit to me at home, I felt Leila dripping sadness. The pressure of her deteriorating relationship with the comrades was going from bad to worse. I sensed that during our short conversation which was punctuated by uncharacteristic sighs that came one after the other. Her visit seemed very short to me. The void was palpable, a void she filled with her flooding sadness. I remained sprawled on the couch studying her sadness that dripped in front of me.

"How's it going?"

"The usual. Nothing new. Just that I came to tell you that I'm getting married the day after tomorrow."

I didn't utter a word. I continued to look at her. I didn't ask. I didn't seek any explanation. I contemplated a deferred love that would get married and come to blame me for letting it slip away. The questions the comrades raised when they learned of the news didn't concern me. I didn't pay any attention to their interpretations. Only Leila concerned me; Leila's presence that fills me. Here it was, slipping away from me. Was it wiped out? Did it go up in smoke?

Leila gives me life, and here she is now, slipping away. That's what I thought. But her marriage could not root her out of me. Leila continued to inhabit me. And Amina kept devoting herself to visiting me. *Her* presence did not have the same flavor as Leila's. Amina furnished all time with her presence, yet the void was extended. As for Leila, she only came in order to be absent. Despite that, there was no time for the void. Leila fills the seconds, every iota of time. I don't know how Amina and I got into it while we were deep in conversation that night when she said,

"Even though my relationship with Leila is limited, and I never feel her direct connection with us, I don't agree with the rumors that were spun against her."

"What do you mean? Who was spinning rumors against her?"

"Latifa and the rest of the comrades, or, some of them, anyway. Latifa told me that Leila had caused a problem between her husband and the comrades, and that her harsh manner was a cover for suspicious practices. 'Leila is a suspicious element.' That's what she said. And that talk isn't so different from what's been said in the yard, even in the discussion circles inside the college. It has really stirred up a lot of hatred. Poor Leila."

"Who exactly said this?"

"Latifa, of course."

"With Mustafa there?"

"No, it was Latifa, Zakia, Aicha, and I. But when Mustafa came home, he sat down with us as the conversation continued. Mustafa didn't confirm or deny it. He sipped his coffee, put his newspaper back under his arm, and left."

Just like that, Mustafa! And you come to me to comment on Leila's marriage? With your tongue twisted in your mouth, lying that losing Leila was too bad, that it was a form of suicide. And you, you're the one who did the killing?!

That night, Amina was relaxed. Darkness began to weave its threads and I understood that she planned on spending the night here. I had no desire for anything. All I was thinking about was going to see Mustafa. I tried to annoy Amina by asking her whether she intended on spending the night here so she would leave and I could go meet him. She just smiled and said, "As you wish."

I went to the bedroom, put on my jacket, grabbed my ID card and keys, and told her I would be back in an hour.

It was a quarter past nine when I caught the last bus to Mustafa's neighborhood. I would have to return home by taxi. I rang the doorbell and heard Latifa's voice coming to me from inside. I had hoped that Mustafa would open the door so I could steal him away to the closest café. I did not have the slightest desire to go through greeting protocols with her. I was still seething. I felt a ringing in my ears.

"Hello, Mouline. Please come in."

"Hi. Is Mustafa here?"

I was obliged to go in. Mustafa was in the bathroom, and I had to wait another fifteen minutes for him. We went into the living room. Latifa sat in front of me. She insisted I drink some tea or coffee, and I insisted that she not go to the trouble. I asked for a glass of water and she brought it to me immediately. As I stared out into space, I noted that the living room was decorated with pictures of martyrs from Mehdi Ben Barka to Che Guevara, as well as some oil paintings lined up in another hall that branched off of the living room we were sitting in. The pictures ran along the edges of the room, and there was a square rug in the middle. It looked magnificent, expensive, and beautiful. It might have been the same rug Mustafa had told us about last year. The one he borrowed money for from all of us. The newspaper editor, Si Ali's driver acted as a middleman for him. He wouldn't have gotten rid of it if it hadn't been velvet. It had been covering the entire area underneath the editor's desk. Latifa could tell I was focusing hard on all these things, and she told me that the paintings were by a painter friend who lived far away, and that he had left them here because of the house's proximity to the galleries. I wasn't as taken by the paintings as I was by Latifa's touch for interior design. Right then, I heard Mustafa clearing his throat as he came in.

"Welcome, welcome. We need dates and milk. Our second home visit since we got married."

Latifa seized upon his words to jeer,

"Meaning you two haven't met since we got married?!"

"No, we're just talking about the house," Mustafa said.

I stood up and pulled at his shoulder a bit, saying,

"I'd like you if just for half an hour, if possible."

"Of course, take the entire night. What do we have? . . . "

"I'd rather go out for a bit."

Mustafa went into the bedroom. Once again, Latifa and I were left sitting face to face. She was chewing some gum. She had knitting needles in her hands and was knitting something grey, a sweater for her husband, perhaps.

Mustafa came out after putting on his coat. I said my good-byes to Latifa and rushed to the door. I couldn't get the image of her clinging to Mustafa out of my head. I could no longer distinguish between Latifa clinging to her master—his guardian par excellence—and between Latifa the woman searching for a position within a specific movement. When she disappeared right after getting married, it began to prove my suspicions about how women who start out as comrades end up captive slaves. Leila was the exception that destroyed all my assumptions.

Mustafa pressed the light-switch, then called the elevator. I asked that we go down the stairs, which he did without comment. Mustafa and Latifa lived on the building's third floor. I was betting that the suffocation I had been feeling inside me would ease. I was hoping that when we arrived at the Café Mona Lisa, I would relax, having gained control of my nerves. I wanted to feel calm when I coolly brought up the subject of Leila. I no longer knew why I was feeling so suffocated. Was it on account of Leila who filled me, or was it that the issue itself had stirred up such awful crushing feelings?

We arrived at the 'B' level and I lit a cigarette. I offered Mustafa one, but he refused, saying,

"No, I quit smoking for good. I won't deny that Latifa, she's the reason. At first, she convinced me I was addicted and had to cut down. Then she said that the budget was off. In the end, she leaned on the fact that it would be unhealthy for the baby we're expecting. And then finally, she found that I wasn't smoking anymore. Can you believe it?"

"But quitting that's motivated by a woman . . . First smoking, then politics!"

Mustafa let out a loud laugh as he pulled the cigarette pack from my hand.

"For this joke, I'll smoke a cigarette."

"No, you'll smoke ten."

We arrived at the Café Mona Lisa. I pulled a chair over for Mustafa, and another for myself. The waiter came over. We ordered two coffees. The café was empty except for four travelers scattered about here and there. The waiter brought our coffees quickly. I paid him and he left. I dove right in, with no introduction.

"I want to know all the rumors *you've* heard about Leila."

"Lots was said, I don't remember what. But Leila's married. What do you care about her now?"

Mustafa knew how much I liked her. He thought I was looking for something about her that would cheer me up.

"So, tell me a little about that 'lots' that you've heard."

"You know that Leila is unclear with the comrades. This is what allows them to take the rumors about her at face value without doing anything to refute them."

"But she's a hundred per cent trustworthy. Do *you* believe everything that's been said about Leila?"

"Of course not, but some doubts have started to settle in my mind."

"For example?"

"She's open to forming relationships with all sorts . . . "

"And this is enough to stab her in the back and fabricate all these scenarios about her? Is having discussions with others a negative thing?"

"But the fact that she's always so elusive gives credence to all of that."

"So, just because the organization doesn't accept her, spinning all those narratives is justified? Even encourages all of that?"

"That's not what I'm saying. That's just my read of a situation."

"But we're the ones benefiting from Leila's activities, by which I mean the party, while she doesn't discuss or refute it. Why didn't one of the comrades discuss the problem with her?"

"And will we designate frameworks to use for clearing the air?"

"But we designate them to muck it up!"

"What do you mean?"

"I mean that Leila was targeted, and the rumors we thought had come from external sources were coming from here, from us. That's what she sensed. It was an attack on her."

"You're blowing this out of proportion. It seems to me that this needs to be contained. Otherwise we'll break into factions. Leila married Mohammed and that's it."

I got up to say goodbye to Mustafa, and intended on bringing the subject up with the comrades. We minimize so many details, but only feel our relationship to the whole when they blow up in our hands, or when they accumulate with other details. Reading how much they have transformed becomes difficult.

We left the café, and I was absolutely sure Mustafa would start to dig into the stream of rumors, underlining my words "coming from here" in red. He would cross-examine Latifa about every tiny point, and about all those other women Leila had spoken directly with about it. When I went to see

Mustafa, I had made the decision to tell him what Amina had said, and make him face reality which would be the beginning of a situation the end of which we would never know. To this day, I don't know how I went down this road with Mustafa. He invited me to spend the night at their place, but after he finally said goodbye and left me on the road, I felt relieved that he did not directly insert Amina into the discussion. I looked at my watch. It was 11:30. It was only then that I remembered Amina so I quickened my pace and threw myself into the first taxi that came by on the main street.

10

I INSERTED THE KEY IN the keyhole. I wanted to apologize, but I found her coming at me wildly with a smile that interceded on my behalf before I could speak. I kissed her. I went into the living room with my hand on the back of her neck. I drew her into my chest. Dinner was laid out on the table and next to it she had placed some bottles of beer. I kissed her and went to wash my hands. I came back and sat on the sofa. Amina lifted the cover off a plate of fish and salad. I jumped up and turned on the television. Amina is the complete opposite of Leila—a woman who is excitingly stable whereas Leila is all over the place, shunning all forms of stability. She told me that the phone had rung twice. Of course, Amina hadn't answered it. That's what I asked ever since she started to visit me, and she complied without ever asking why. When I lifted my eyes up to Amina, I noticed that she had put on rose-colored eye shadow and lipstick. I looked at her closely. I examined her. She felt it and lowered her head, arranging the salad on my plate. For the first time, I fixed my gaze on her face and realized she was very beautiful. Amina is like a piece of ice, but it is Leila who burns inside of me. Amina is beautiful and she is here. Leila is the one that I need, but she is there, perhaps still all wound up in her shyness, sharing a bed with Mohammed. Unlike Amina, I really wanted to eat. She distracted herself by playing with the lettuce leaves. She cut them into little pieces without serving herself. I finished eating, pulled myself back a little, then moved over to the wide sofa close to the television. Amina got right up. She brought the plates to the kitchen, wiped the table, then took her glass and sat down to relax next to me. She threw her head onto my thigh after putting her right hand underneath her head. I played with her hair with one hand while holding my glass in the other. She finished her drink and lit a cigarette. She started to smoke as she rubbed against my body. I reached my hand toward the glass and Amina brought it closer to me. An image of Leila rose up from the abyss.

When we met to finish a special issue of the poster-magazine at the college, I was in my last year, and Leila was in her second. The article was to appear at the start of the following week. I arrived at the Café Chateaubriand and found that she had arrived a few minutes before me. I apologized and sat down. The waiter came over. I ordered a beer and Leila ordered some tea. I took the newspapers and flipped through them again. I put them aside. She pulled her purse over. She took out a small notepad and some magazines we would need for proof. She put them back in the purse. She lifted her head to me and then lowered it to the notepad. I sensed that something was happening but I didn't know what. I sensed that she was upset. I noticed her turn toward the counter more than three times. The café was teeming with people. I asked her if she wanted to get the waiter to hurry up before we began.

"You want me to be frank? Get the waiter over here quickly and cancel the beer. Have a tea or coffee."

She said it then lowered her eyes to the pages of the notepad, her face turning red.

She had been with us for two years, but for the first time, I realized how young Leila seemed. I got the waiter, changed my order, and told him to hurry up a little.

I didn't ask her for an explanation. I imagined the comrades, had they been here, would have gone on and on about it for a while even though deep down they preferred this woman who was still wrapped in the shyness of years when her face got red, or when it was difficult to easily take her in. Leila put the newspapers aside and pushed the glass of tea to the edge of the table. She took out a pile of paper and placed half of it in front of me and the other half in front of herself.

We were dealing with the most recent Palestinian incident and its coverage in the Arab media, specifically magazines. We began an initial inventory of the magazines and divided them into piles of monthlies and journals. After that, we moved on to the size of the incident's coverage in each magazine, then to the nature of how it was treated. Leila didn't need this whole bibliography. We had agreed six months ago that we would follow up when the magazine's annual program was drawn up. She put a small notepad down in front of us that she kept checking in order to verify the dates and titles of the articles, and to arrange their citations. As for each articles' contents, she jotted those down in brief, condensed points. I was drawn to how neatly and efficiently she worked. I was embarrassed as I gently removed my bunch of oversized papers from between the ribs of the magazines.

We worked for three hours straight. When we finished the essay and reviewed it, it was clear that the one magazine that was dear to my heart had inadvertently been dropped from the analysis. Leila laughed as she commented on the intentional omission that would transform into an open ending. She said it as she lifted her body up off the chair. She looked at her watch, said goodbye, and left. I stayed behind. I ordered a beer, and then another as I contemplated Leila and the rustle of her shadow that had begun to creep into me.

I grabbed Amina's wrist to look at her watch. She put her cigarette down and raised her hand up to my mouth. I kissed it. I plunged my nose into her palm and looked at the watch again. I turned off the television and we went to bed. I changed my clothes while Amina headed to the bathroom. She came back and took off everything. She put on my summer pajamas and sprayed perfume all over her body, then slipped into bed. I turned out the light. I flung myself over to her side. I embraced her. I passed my lips over her mouth. The smell of toothpaste burned me which reminded me that I hadn't brushed my teeth. Amina was a master of all the erotic arts. I wondered how she had learned it all, but didn't dare get into it with her. I feared the consequences of asking for indulgences I had no desire of receiving.

Amina always speaks in a hybrid language—half Arabic, half French. Her pronunciation of each one is sound, although I prefer it when she speaks Arabic. She surprised me one evening, saying,

"Leila's complicated."

"How so?"

"In her relationship to men."

"Who told you that?"

"Once, when I was visiting Latifa, Leila came to pick up some printed material that Mustafa had left for her. We talked about the relationship. Latifa told us that she was trying to get Mustafa to quit smoking even though she couldn't stand kissing a mouth that didn't smell like tobacco. We all laughed. Latifa asked Leila what she thought, and her face reddened as she answered, 'When I try it, I'll let you know.'"

"Latifa replied that she should start with a mouth that had kissed a cigarette before kissing her, as long as she hadn't tried it yet. Leila laughed and got up. Latifa gave her the printed materials Mustafa had left for her and she walked out."

Leila seemed like an ancient wine, as old as Father Yiannaros. She came to me unexpectedly. Putting the dream around my palm. How do I flow with life while she blazes like a rustling cypress tree with her childlike face? How many women do I need in order to get to Leila? How many women do I need in order to embrace her or even to know her? This woman, desired by the five senses, but never attained.

We woke up the next morning to the telephone ringing. Amina went off to the bathroom. I grabbed the receiver and heard Abbas's voice, which I can easily distinguish from all others.

"I called you twice yesterday, but no one answered. Did you forget our appointment?"

"No, I didn't forget. I'll explain when we meet."

I turned toward the bathroom. Amina was still in the shower. The sound of splashing water echoed out to me.

"Look, Abbas, maybe we can meet here at my place tonight. Call Kamal and tell him."

"What time?"

"Name it."

"How about eight?"

"Okay. You'll find the key in its usual spot."

"Under the router."

"That's right."

Amina came out of the shower. She headed to the bedroom, her lower half covered with a small towel. Her polished, ivory back stirred a desire in me to join her there. She threw the towel aside and grabbed her pants and sweater. I took a step back, then turned toward the bathroom. I went out to the living room and found that she had put down two cups of coffee and some slices of French toast.

Amina still had no appetite. She made do with half a cup of coffee, then lit a cigarette and scrutinized me as I wolfed down what was left of the toast. She put her cigarette out in the ashtray. She grabbed her handbag from on top of the sofa and got up to say goodbye.

"Until next time. I'll be gone five days."

"Is everything okay?"

"I received a letter from my family letting me know that my mother is sick. I'm traveling to see her in a little over an hour on the 9 o'clock train."

I walked Amina to the door. I kissed her. She said goodbye and left. It seemed best not to broach the subject of her not coming back tonight. I went into the bedroom, grabbed my keys and ID, and rushed out. That was no more than a few minutes after Amina left. But this was our routine. We had implicitly agreed not to go in or out together. We might be together for three straight days, but when we headed out, each one of us left alone. Amina continued to visit me this way until she turned to Abbas and they got married. She didn't tell me about that directly. I only found out from Abbas, then from the comrades. To this day I don't know whether the woman revealed all the details to her husband after they got married. Did Amina tell Abbas about her frequent visits to me and our nights together? I don't know.

I came home after seven that evening. I had left the housekey for Abbas and Kamal under the router. I rang the doorbell. Abbas's voice came to me from inside. He opened the door and yelled behind him,

"We'll eat dinner here!"

I handed him the package of kofta and vegetables and took out the beer and wine. I hurried to put them down on the living room table to rest my hand while Abbas went into the kitchen where he put the rest of the packages.

I had missed Kamal. I gave him a warm hug. The three of us chatted a bit. I realized that I had forgotten to buy bread. Abbas went out to get it and Kamal and I went into the kitchen. He told me about some comrades who were coming to join us, to complete their studies at the university, and about his initial calls with them. He told me about four of them from Leila's city, and that they had asked about her as soon as they arrived.

That was enough for me to get into the subject of her with Kamal, but I thought it would be more appropriate for all three of us to be there, so we discussed it right after dinner. It was clear that Kamal had a lot of reservations about what had been said against her, and he did not understand why some of the comrades were attacking her. I knew right then that I had made a huge mistake when I spoke with Mustafa about Latifa having leaked some private information. I went back over the matter from the beginning with Kamal and Abbas. They were uneasy. Kamal confirmed that the attack against Leila was no more than a reaction that all of us, including ourselves, were involved in by remaining silent all this time. We went over the problem from every angle. Kamal was an even-keeled friend whom I respect a lot. Abbas suggested a way to deal with the problem and salvage what could be saved. Kamal didn't agree because, in his view, the solution held one side to account, and the other to be rehabilitated. And Leila might see the clarification and apology as coming way too late, whereas we didn't know what holding the other side accountable would reveal, especially since the problem extended to more than one city. Kamal was like that with everything, like a candle burning at both ends.

"So, what do you suggest?"

"Let's think. Perhaps we can task one of us with calling Leila and extending a bridge to her. Casually, outside of any specific orientation. The important thing is that we contain these sorts of problems in the future. They don't always have to get so huge."

Abbas glanced at his watch as he cursed Mustafa who had brought us back to square one. Kamal confirmed that the problem was not so simple. Rather, it reflected the lack of communication there had been between us before we were opened up to any other level. That's how the discussion concerning Leila led to other subjects of an internal nature which we mulled over for the rest of the night.

11

As suddenly as my intimate relationship with Leila began, it ended. Neither one of us could unearth the other anymore. Her body was boiling hot underneath mine. At that moment, I seemed like a madman. Like someone who has found water after seeing a desert mirage. Leila was my water. A woman wrapped up in the shyness of years. Just sensing that was enough to kindle the desire within me. Slipping toward her. Plunging into her. Then conquering her. I wanted to inhabit her. To sweep her up and never let her go. At first, she felt boiling hot, but after a little bit, she turned into a piece of ice. I asked her to move. I would moan, and Leila would move her head out from under me. I pleaded with her, and when my eyes drowned in hers, I found a look that was begging me to stop.

Impossible, Leila. I can't. I would explode immediately if I left you now. Bear with me for just a little bit, I beg of you. Bear with me.

That was the only time I caught hold of Leila's body.

"I want to dive deep inside you," I said.

"You see depths. Maybe all I have is surface."

"Right now, I'm fine with the surface of depth."

"How could you reach the depth anyway?"

"Are you a virgin?"

"Are you?"

Thus, Leila slapped me with her answer. I crumpled into my deluded question. That's how Leila was. *I* serve her some sticky water, and she offers me up a drop of the water of life. She slipped out from underneath my body and went to the bathroom. Now, I only see Leila by accident or in a narrow street or wide boulevards in my imagination. I no longer see Leila, and she won't come visit me at home anymore until all that water has dried up. We almost forget that we had intertwined our bodies that day. If only one of us could visit the other in a normal and deep way. But it is a way that no longer possesses the boldness to scratch the surface of what is deep, or dig into the depths of what is shallow.

Leila visited me in Gharbia. After I became accustomed to her visits, and after we had extended our hearts toward one another, I decided to delve into that day we never started together. Because I forgot to forget the day I tasted her. I inserted my tongue into her mouth. She laughed, her tongue playing with mine. And as she tickled my earlobe and the back of my neck, I shivered excitely. I wanted to devour her. I asked her why she had seemed so hot that day, then after that, became as cold as a piece of ice.

"Your roar frightened me and the bed's squeaking bothered me . . . "

I exploded into laughter when I heard Leila's response. I remembered the metal bed and how it squeaked whenever two bodies rubbed up against one another on it. I wondered, did all women, every one of them, notice the squeak, or was it just Leila? Amina writhed around underneath my body on request like a slaughtered bird. She was never bothered by the bed's noise. I asked Leila what she meant by my roar.

"You would make frightening sounds that resembled a lion's roar. Or, more like the moaning of a still standing victim with a knife plunged in his back. I pictured you falling dead on top of me."

"You don't have to imagine anything like that from now on."

"With Mohammed, the same thing happens. You're all the same."

For the first time, Leila revealed something about her life with Mohammed. I wanted more, but who would dare ask for that? I became aware of the smell of her perfume and said,

"That day, I absolutely loved your perfume. I dowsed myself in it. And now?"

She smiled and her eyes dropped to the ground.

"You all love us, for our perfume, for the fire inside us. You bet everything on something that you've been grabbing onto from the start. A body. Perfume. The burning fire . . . whatever. As for us, we need to put up with you without a concrete bet. Imagine that whenever my body is entwined with Mohammed's, he takes me into his arms. He embraces me. And when he buries my head in his neck and takes in my entire body, I don't smell perfume or flowers. I smell rust. I began to accept the smell of rust, and then I began to love it. Now I love the smell of rust. Imagine that!"

Where did all of this power to discourage come from, Leila? Even though Leila told me what she considered to be details about her relationship with Mohammed, from what she told me, I didn't feel that she was allowing me the chance to get into it as I wanted to. All I wanted to know was how she had been convinced to marry Mohammed despite the fact that they had never had any sort of a relationship before. Mohammed was in his last year when Leila enrolled in the college. He was the first to pay attention to her and he continued to pursue her with his love and desire to connect with her. Mohammed was not engaged with a specific political line, but he moved around the university with a serious political consciousness. Even though his connection to political work faded as soon as he got a job, his relations with everyone remained cordial. Thus, after five years of pursuing her, Mohammed married Leila, betting on a woman who possessed so much potential for slipping away. He was not in the slightest bit prepared for Leila to continue along the same path after getting married. He wanted to mold her according to the type he had started to design for himself and his life. He was not at all pleased with the project she surprised all of us with. Mohammed was the last one to find out that Leila had opened up Moukhtar's case so she could pore over its details. He did not know until after she had finished preparing all aspects of the case, topping it off by traveling to see his children to discuss how they felt about their father's detention. Moukhtar's case was a tale told by seven different tongues. I don't know how Leila came up with the idea to look into it. She never came to visit me without a thick file folder under her arm. She surprised me with it, and I tried to make her aware that publishing the file under these specific circumstances was something that would irritate a lot of people. Even the party that considered Moukhtar a member was unprepared to dig into his case right then.

"But how did you manage to conduct the conversation?"

"You'll know later."

"And does Mohammed know about it?"

"Why would he know? We never agreed that we would always necessarily be happy with what the other one did."

I stared at Leila for a long time and asked her how Moukhtar was doing, to which she responded,

"That man is pure gold, for sure."

Moukhtar was thrown onto Gharbia's death row eight years ago. The party never took a position concerning him. That was too much for many members of the youth organization at the time, as well as the party leadership. The question we continued to mull over and discuss was whether Moukhtar had been engaged in a party mission. It was the burning question on everyone's mind, but the leadership did not provide a response. Could Moukhtar have been so meticulous planning all that by himself, taking on the role of general secretary and council president as well? And through their loaded questions, they insisted on revealing the network that had planned for an assassination scenario. Moukhtar had taken refuge in the region of Imzi to work as a sharecropper with one of the well-off families there. Their wealth did not come from work though, or even by way of inheritance, but rather, by benefitting through service to the colonizer. But how could Moukhtar distinguish which of the two twin brothers had infiltrated a group of organization members? And how could he continue to look into the twins' faces for eight months and scrutinize the details of all the connections and confirm that the suspicious element was now occupying the position of regional Caid? But he executed the rest of the plan with exceptional steadiness and conviction. Of course, after being on the run for a while and not being able to leave the country, Moukhtar was arrested and brought before the military court. Did he receive any party guidance that allowed him to appear so calm and composed at the trial during which the defense also revealed that an operation to get rid of the agent was a personal one that Moukhtar had undertaken on his own? And as much as the defense emphasized Moukhtar's party membership, it confirmed that the operation was planned by him alone, in exchange for his exoneration by the party.

When we arrived at the central prison, we knew Moukhtar was languishing on death row, and we didn't fully absorb what that meant until after having lived it up close. For a prisoner to be sitting on death row is enough to tear the soul from the body in little bits. Just being there meant a slow death that mocked all parts of the body every day, without allowing it to give up the ghost. It is a double-terror, where the death sentence is hung on the occupant's forehead as sure as night hangs on the edge of dawn. Every day the detainee is dragged out for the sentence to be executed, it is put off until the following day. Thus, they come every day with chains and a fat bunch of keys jangling in their hands. Then, they walk through seven doors before getting to the last one. During all of this, the keys clang and echo for Moukhtar to hear. Execution was a ritual that put you on high alert for days and years. So, despite its repetition on each successive day, there was no way of putting a sheen on its brutality. A ritual that lives by killing the one living there. Imagine, every night thinking it will be your last. You don't sleep. Rather, your memory will race with you to search its cellars for those who have settled there from the beginning, as well as those who joined them right before the end. Then you close your eyes just a little bit in order to see this thin self in relation to the mechanism of repression that harvests what remains of the blood in your veins and heart. And in the end, you will long for just this self to remain. You long for it, and it only, to ward off a slow death.

When she came with his thick case file in her hands, Leila told me that he had asked her to prepare him some liver cutlets (which is what she did) and send them to him with his daughter, Aicha. It was the first time I had heard that Moukhtar had sons and daughters. That was through Leila.

When Moukhtar learned that we were in Gharbia prison too, he insisted on seeing me. He was aware of my close relationship with Leila. He insisted that we meet in the prison yard so he could ask me about details specific to her and what she had been subjected to following the file's publication. But if Moukhtar had been looking forward to learning some of the details, I'm the one who learned from him. Leila wouldn't grant but a tiny bit of what you might be seeking from her. But Leila, the one who doesn't cry, cried here in prison. In fact, the only place I can imagine her crying was here in prison. When she visited Moukhtar, they embraced like old friends who had been living far away from one another, and she broke out crying. It was Moukhtar's first visit outside of the limited number of times his children had come to see him. Her visit was priceless. That's how Moukhtar put it.

She surprised me as she passed along greetings from my nieces and nephews, each one by name. Leila is extremely spontaneous and profoundly deep at the same time. I was painfully transparent with her. I am sure that I felt the systematic persecution some members of the party had forced on her more than the agony that was attached to my own case.

"Leila is a woman, my brother, and the party should be proud enough that a woman like Leila can be counted among those who stood with it. Do you know what it is that'll allow this woman to inhabit me until the end of my life?" asked Moukhtar.

"What's that?"

"Her stability. Leila is clear-headed. Despite everything that's been done to her, many of those who attacked her have begun to die off, yet she's still here, at the core of our suffering. She bandages our wounds and she is the wound."

When we joined the organization, we truly believed Leila would be the first to applaud the project and that she'd join us immediately. Especially since the organization's plan had recruited women in its political program by criticizing the negative and marginal positions they held inside the party. But the opposite happened. Leila remained cool to the idea. She scrutinized me as I explained our project to her so I could end all my analyses by asking her what she thought.

"We may agree and share the same opinions, but I can't join so easily, just like that."

"It's just a matter of being convinced, not of joining or entering or leaving."

"When you all joined the party, didn't you also have to be convinced?"

"But we weren't compelled to interact with a framework, like a totem we'd worship day and night. Developments on the ground require another alternative vision . . ."

"I'm not talking about worshipping a totem, but I always start things out by necessarily exhausting all possibilities in crystallizing our proposals and developing them inside the same framework. And I believe that this step, the step of exhausting the discussion inside the party hasn't been completed yet."

Our discussion branched out in more than one direction, and I remained perplexed by Leila's fixed positions. Perhaps I see her now from here, from prison, with positions that seem more fixed than they did in the moment when she first expressed them. We were, at the time, hot as embers. We saw ourselves only with youthful vigor. We experienced ebbs and flows toward others. I was excited as I confronted Leila with the party's reform positions from the most recent stage and its truce negotiations. When I remembered what the comrades had said about her, I understood quickly when I saw the glint of her tired eyes that were dripping sadness. She closed them as if swallowing a bitter pill. I apologized. And she responded to me, still chewing on my words,

"This is a reality, but you know that I'm not an expert in forming reactions. I'm sure the greatest thing standing in our way isn't the police or the Makhzen. It isn't this backwardness that surrounds us. Rather, it's comrades who are experts in standing in the way of other comrades. And if one of us needs to stand firm in the face of all of these machinations, then we're required to stand firm, doubly-firm, in the face of back-stabbing of comrades, or quasi-comrades. I don't know. The important thing is that, when everyone is feeling pessimistic, one comrade turns to another and says, 'Come on. Let's play the game of despair together.' So, I was a temporary target. Tomorrow, it could be you or someone else. I don't know . . . "

"But people, aren't *they* the principles?"

"I've said this to myself more than once. What I needed most was to keep myself together. But between you and me, I no longer trust principles that don't walk on solid ground . . . "

Leila said this as she lowered her eyes, as if telling me the discussion was over and that she had no desire to continue. For the first time I felt that what linked me to this Leila could not possibly be erased or disappear. It was here, making its way through all my pores. Leila is a woman who teaches you how you can live differences to their extremes, not only out of belief, but out of respect. Leila fills me. She fills me up. That's how, that day, I broke through her shyness, gathered up all my courage to get close to her, grabbed her hand, and . . .

When Moukhtar asked me for details about Leila's detention after she published his file, I found myself barely able to mumble some bits of information. She hadn't delved into the details about her days in the secret detention center and I was unable to break through all that self-composure. I was betting that the story would flow all by itself as soon as I visited her, seeing as how close we were. Mohammed opened the door. I greeted him warmly. He brought me to the salon where Leila was lying down on a single bed at the far end of the room. I went in and found her lying on her back. Mohammed went in before me. He shook her a little. She got up and turned toward me. Her eyes were filled with tears which she did not wipe away. I embraced her warmly. She gathered herself together. She raised the pillow a bit, her lower half remaining underneath the covers. I asked her about what was going on, about her health. She answered tersely. Mohammed was there, sitting on the sofa facing us. I sat on the sofa close to Leila. She asked me what I might drink. She cast a glance at Mohammed who stood up and reasked the question. After they insisted, I asked for a coffee and Mohammed loped off to the kitchen to prepare it. I repeated my questions to Leila, but her answers remained curt. I thought that Mohammed leaving the room might encourage her to start talking, but she maintained her silence. She asked me how things were going and about the general direction of the organization. The party was still making progress, but I had never been concerned with this when I spoke to Leila. She told me that some party comrades had called Mohammed at work and informed him of their desire to visit as soon as she got out. I looked at her, a revealing smile forming on her lips.

Leila knew that my connection to those who had been comrades of mine in the party had ended as soon as I joined the organization. Therefore, I didn't dare ask her opinion of what they had suggested. Mohammed came back in. He put my cup of coffee and a glass of water down in front of me. He offered Leila a glass of water with mint. He walked out only to come back in after having gotten dressed. He said goodbye and left for work after giving Leila a kiss on the forehead. In spite of all of these suggestions that the situation was normal, I felt a sort of suffocation the whole time Mohammed was sitting with us. He didn't utter a word, but rather punctuated his time sitting there with groans, opening the newspaper in front of him and turning the pages in an attempt to cover up the sounds he was making. I asked her about how much this was all affecting Mohammed. She sighed, then answered,

"Trust me, Mouline, I'm not at all ready to dredge up those pains. They're like all the other the wounds I have all over my body. I'm not at all prepared to think about that. I'll allow time to make it easier to deal with."

That's how I found out, in passing, that Leila's body was carrying wounds. I felt her ruin. She was not prepared to discuss anything at all. I recommended that she take good care of her health and stood up to say goodbye. This is why I couldn't come up with anything to tell Moukhtar about the details of Leila's confinement in the secret police station. And I didn't tell him anything about how ruined she was. It was clear how fond he was of her, so I left it that way, open until Leila started to visit me here in prison after she had split up with Mohammed. Moukhtar was the happiest one of all about the connection between us. He's "pure gold" as Leila put it.

12

ALTHOUGH IN PRISON, ONE DAY is like the next, I sensed that that day was not going to be like the others. I went to sleep late the previous night and woke up early. I immediately turned on the radio. I pulled the water jug over from the corner of the cell and gulped down what was in it. I felt a burning. I didn't know why, nor did I know how to lessen it. And I felt an emptiness opening up inside me and throughout my cell. The emptiness frightened me, so I went back to my bed. I twisted and turned, right and left, then onto my belly. I stuck my hand under the pillow. I grew tired of trying to distract myself to fill the endless void. I jumped up as if stung by a scorpion. I took off my pajamas. I put on my tracksuit and rushed out to the prison yard. Perhaps I could regain some mental repose by getting some fresh air. I entered the yard. As usual, I found Moha walking around in a circle like someone who had been hit on the head. I greeted him and as usual, he did not respond. Then I started to run around the yard, trying to avoid looking at him. I was growing tired of Moha. He was an endless pain. As soon as you encountered him, the pain churned inside you. I felt the blood starting to course through my veins. I sped up so that I might regain something of my physical and mental vigor. It was bright and clear here, totally unlike my cell, but a sort of suffocation still enveloped the place, bearing down on my soul. I saw Moha start to leave the yard and head toward the cells. I watched him without his being aware. He was dragging his legs as if they weren't his. I wondered if that was the result of walking around in too many circles. I continued to stare at him. Then I ran in place. When Moha got to the entrance, he stopped. I sensed him turn his body, rather, his head back toward the yard. I lowered my gaze and continued to run in place to try to avoid his. I started moving my neck around so I could lift my head up and confirm that he had left, but I was surprised to see that he was still fixed in place, waiting for me to nod at him. I stopped running to wait and see what he wanted from me. He raised his hand in greeting and smiled, then he turned toward the door and disappeared. I stood where I was, baffled. Moha never talked to anyone, nor did he smile at anyone. As shocked as he was being here among us, he always had a calm look about him. He never cared that we were in the yard, even if it was filled with us. Except we always saw him avoiding Ahmed Choufan's eyes. Often, I would watch him from a distance as he grumbled about seeing Choufan. He felt a certain disgust, and would quickly turn his face to the wall.

Moha disappeared entirely from view. I continued to run. I felt the sweat dripping all over my body. Then I stopped. The prison bathroom was still out of order. I filled a bucket with cold water and took off my clothes, shivering despite how hot my body was. I went back to my cell and felt a desire to sleep, so I put off eating breakfast. I got into my still unmade bed. I pulled just the sheet over my body and fell into a deep sleep out of which I was pulled by an alarming commotion pierced by screaming and loud voices in the corridor. Then Salah, pale, burst into my cell.

"Come, Mouline, come. Moha, Moha . . ."

The words tumbled out of his mouth. I got up as he pulled me by the shoulder. We headed to Moha's cell in front of which the comrades, the prison guards, and the administration were all crowded. No one was looking into the cell. All of them had either closed their eyes or turned their heads. I pushed some of the comrades away and walked inside slowly. Oh, I wish I hadn't! Moha was hanging from a rope. His body seemed long, his tongue longer. Dangling like laundry hung out to dry in the dark.

Ahmed Choufan, the one standing closest to Moha's body, stood underneath his dangling feet and screamed at the top of his lungs,

"Why, Moha?! Why?!"

I gasped and felt nauseous. I wanted to puke my guts out. I rushed outside. The smell of death wafted over the place and wrapped itself around the entire prison. I recalled an image of Moha from this morning. I recalled him smiling and waving to me, and I was overtaken with nausea once again. Oh! Had I known what he had in store, I would have held onto him in the yard.

But how did Moha get up to the top of the cell's window to attach the rope? That was the unanswered question that made its way around. Did someone help Moha commit suicide? There was only a chair in the cell, but even if he had stood on it, he would not have been able to tie the rope to the top of the five bars of the cell's window, the small window up at the ceiling. He would need a ladder to do that, but only the prison administration had a ladder, and it was only on rare occasions that we would borrow it to look for a book on the upper shelves of the library. That was always done in the presence of one of the prison guards. As soon as we found the book, the guard would return the ladder to the administration.

Police investigators arrived with the new warden trembling in front of them. He had just been appointed head of the prison four months prior when the Commander was transferred to a new prison that had been experiencing intense protests. The country's prisons were swamped. But for the first time, the new prison was filled with people who had risen up from the masses. Moha's suicide was considered by the new warden (for whom we kept the name, the Commander) a bad omen. He did not hide his anxiety, nor his cursing of Moha, who had marked his promotion to the post of warden with a suicide.

All the information was written down and he picked up the chair that had been kicked to the floor. We moved away from the cell, filling the corridor, then the yard with our roaring protest. They did not ask us to move away from Moha's cell, but it wasn't easy to watch while they loosened the noose from his neck.

The coroner arrived. The first thing he did was remove Moha's pants to check whether the death was the result of an actual suicide, or murder then hanging. That required an examination of Moha's sexual organ; if there was semen there, it would be a confirmed suicide. Sexual desire accompanies men until they die, so sperm is squeezed out by the violence of death by hanging. That's what the doctor told us as he wrote out his pathological report on Moha.

It was eleven in the morning, which is what prodded the prison administration to rush the burial. We protested as loudly as we could about this decision. Moha should not be buried until after his family had been informed. The Commander made it clear that since taking over the prison's administration, he hadn't seen anyone visit Moha. We knew Moha was cut off from his family tree. No one visited him except for his grey-haired mother! The woman burned with sadness and cried nonstop until she lost most of her sight and stopped coming to visit altogether. We knew that the postman didn't reach Moha's village and letters only arrived haphazardly on Mondays. However, we took a chance on our families, our girlfriends, and other people we knew. They had to attend Moha's funeral which the administration had begun to insist pass in absolute secrecy and total silence. After some back and forth, and after their total refusal to delay burying Moha's corpse that same day, our voices rose high into the sky as the warden felt more constrained and restless. Salah asked the prison warden to allow him to make a phone call from his office. The warden opened his mouth and granted the request if only it could put out the fire. Salah called Souad at her family's house and told her about Moha's suicide, and that the administration was going to bury him that day. He insisted that she inform the families who were close by.

Salah returned, assuring us that they would come. I don't know why we felt such shame that Moha would be conveyed to his final resting place surrounded only by prison guards. The burial rites had to be performed within the necessary confines of custom. No more than an hour and a half passed before crowds of families who lived close to Gharbia arrived at the prison. Lalla Aicha came carrying the shroud, embalming herbs, oud al-qamari wood, and rose water. She was a woman who was always prepared. She told us that, no sooner did she receive the news did she convey it to her neighbor, who insisted that she bring Moha a piece of Meccan shroud. The prison administration brought in the faqih and two body washers. We insisted that Abou Abid go in with them, so he did after Oum Khalid handed him the parcel containing the shroud, the rose water, and the embalming supplies. We brought out our mattresses and put them down on the ground for the families to sit on. Souad arrived with her belly extending out in front of her; she was in the final days of her ninth month. She had stopped visiting Salah two months prior at the insistence of the doctor, who told her not to travel as she needed to stay on her back for the final two months because the fetus was in a descended position close to the cervix. That's what Salah told me. Souad came with Rabia, bringing bread, dates, dried figs, and olives. They also brought alms for the dead in two baskets. Salah rushed to Souad, hugged her, and took the basket from her. I asked her about Leila, and she told me that she had gone to the courthouse to attend a trial hearing of members of the party's central committee. Souad had left a note under her door informing her of Moha's death. Even though I had been following the party schism through Leila, I had forgotten the trial date.

We stood as comrades, and for the first time in years, we stood together rather than in groups. We were dripping sadness over the loss of Moha. Ahmed Choufan looked pale, like someone running from death, or the grave. We all felt the loss, and we felt it twice as much, tangibly so, when Moha's body was brought out. We stood in one row, each of us bending down to kiss his head that was wrapped in the shroud. It was a farewell kiss. Ahmed Choufan was hesitant to say goodbye when his turn came. He slipped out of the line and furtively inserted himself further back. That's how he put it off until he found himself standing there all alone. We could hear our families' wailing despite everyone's efforts to hold their tongues. But the sight of Ahmed Choufan as he stepped slowly and deliberately toward Moha's head made us burst into tears. When Ahmed leaned toward Moha's head, kissing it, and rolling his face over it, he wept, keening and begging Moha to forgive him.

Oum Khalid let out two trills despite how hoarse her voice was. We turned toward her, roused by the sound. She said,

"My dear children, Moha deserves three trills, just like a bridegroom."

Then she pulled herself together, barely getting out a third trill for a groom who had never seen a wedding or a bride. By God, Moha, it would have been easier had you been the victim of a frivolous woman, not a present-day revolutionary . . .

The funeral procession set off with the prison warden in front, followed by the faqih, the vice-warden, and Abou Abid. Walking behind them were the rest of the family members who had come, more than fourteen families. Salah insisted that Souad stay behind in light of how precarious her situation was, but she refused. Her eyes looked swollen from all the crying. Everyone left and *we* stayed behind. Ahmed Choufan continued to weep as he had never wept for a man before. We tried to bandage the wound, but we needed a bandage that was as strong as the grief. There wasn't enough time for the families to return to us, but we weren't expecting *every-one* who accompanied Moha to come to us the following day. Souad didn't come. She was conveyed directly from the cemetery to the hospital in an ambulance. All of those who came hurled words like hot coals. We had never seen our families so riled up. As soon as we learned the reason, we blew up as we never had before. They had encircled Moha's grave with chains because he had not yet completed his sentence. The chains would remain around the grave until the sentence was served. The new warden tried to convince us that the matter had nothing to do with him or with the prison administration. It came from above and there was nothing new in it. In fact, it was customary practice for regular prisoners. That's what the warden said, and that's how they forced our families to end the visit as we stood in the corridor and continued to protest the chains. It had been a long time since we had come together in unified protest about something. We felt the heat flowing through us that evening. The following day, the subject of two newspaper headlines was Moha's suicide and his imprisonment in chains following his burial. We drafted a communiqué which started with us mourning Moha and ended with a protest of the chains.

A week passed. The issue began to lose steam, but Moha's spirit continued to hover over us and sprinkle us with an overwhelming sadness so intense it did not diminish until Souad gave birth. She had stayed in the recovery room for a week after Moha's burial. The doctor said that if she had arrived another hour later, it would have been stillborn.

News of Souad having given birth was enough to give the atmosphere a relatively more pleasant air. Salah could not have been happier. He practically flew to the hospital to see his son three days later. The administration hadn't learned of Souad's pregnancy until the day of Moha's death. One of the guards asked me whether Souad had gotten divorced from Salah and remarried. I ignored his question, not knowing how to respond, especially since my frank answer might reveal the recipe to the others. All I could do was ignore him and walk away.

Salah returned from visiting Souad, still carrying the fragrance of his child on his lips and nose, and in his eyes too. We kissed. He wanted to rub some of that fragrance off on us.

"What are you going to name him, Salah?"

"Samad. Yes, I'll name him Samad."

Many comrades and friends outside the prison named their new children Samad. All we had left was to dress our children in the names of our martyrs. There was Omar, Mehdi, Samad, Amine, Abdellatif, Saïda, Zubaida, all walking around as children in front of us. We watched Samad grow as Souad brought him once every two weeks. The administration, humiliated, would not allow a child to come in to visit his father in prison because prison law forbade that. They were scared for the psychological state of our children. That's what they said. But after an extensive back and forth, Souad brought little Samad in to us. We all gathered around and kissed him. In him we breathed in a childhood we had been cut off from. We felt Salah's yearning for Samad and his mother, Oum Samad. We left them to themselves after preparing a pot of tea and offering them some cookies we had collected from what we had left. Samad grew in front of us. We saw him first as a plan sketched out by Salah for us in the cell, then as a fetus carried by Souad in her belly, and now flesh and blood, nursing and crying and smiling. Samad grew before our eyes. But five years later, he would start to come with his uncle when Souad withdrew from Salah's life after requesting a divorce. To this day, Salah has not explained why they separated. In fact, he swears on all that has passed and all that might come to be that he doesn't know. It only began when her visits became less frequent, and Salah started to ask for an explanation. Then came the breaks that lasted almost a month. Salah continued to insist on an explanation, only for things to come to a head with Souad requesting a divorce. Salah grudgingly agreed, and was surprised after just three and a half months by Souad's remarriage.

It was a violent blow to Salah's very existence. It plunged him into a terrifying silence for more than a year. Only his son, Samad, could fill his heart and put a temporary smile on his face with each visit.

I don't know why Moukhtar insisted on seeing me. He had passed word to me through Allal, the guard. Moukhtar only saw the prison yard once every twenty days, which was the day he urged Allal to allow us to meet. The yard was our refuge from the confinement of the cell. The guards no longer kept us from meeting up with Moukhtar. But it wasn't just that. Today was the day Leila was coming to visit, so I was between a rock and a hard place. Should I go out to the prison yard to meet Moukhtar, or should I wait here in the corridor for Leila to come? I went out to Moukhtar and he clarified that he actually wanted to see Leila. We arranged things with Allal, giving him everything we could. Ever since I stopped smoking, I gave him what came to me. He smiled and pretended not to notice as Moukhtar and I walked in his direction to enter the corridor from the yard. I brought out an additional mattress and laid it on the floor next to the mattress Leila and I would sit on. The meeting was to happen in the square spot, but we brought the mattress from the mihrab to the corridor, and Abid gathered up *his* mattress as he clapped and laughed, and placed it in the mihrab. Leila arrived and her face lit up when she saw Moukhtar. Leila looks like a child when she's happy. They embraced warmly as he put his arms around her and repeated loudly,

"Are you still being stubborn?"

She smiled and arranged all of her face's features without them forming a look that could be interpreted as positive or negative.

Moukhtar laughed, pulling at her hands and sitting down on the floor. Leila realized that she hadn't hugged me. I felt like a neglected child, but she came to my rescue, letting go of his hand and coming forward to embrace me. I kissed her and the three of us sat down. It seemed that Moukhtar wanted to see Leila so he could learn about the details of the trial of the enemy brothers in the party, and about the entire case. I felt like a third wheel. I excused myself to go to my cell to prepare tea. Leila asked for black tea, as usual, and I made green tea for Moukhtar. I tried to take my time so they could finish up their discussion about private internal matters, but when I came back, Leila asked me why I had taken so long. Without the least bit of reservation, the discussion between them flowed as if it were just getting started.

I asked her what the other parties thought about the situation.

"Everyone expressed regret in their public statements after they had cheered and applauded it inside their headquarters."

For the first time I felt Leila showing her bias for something, running away from defending something else. But Moukhtar continued to turn the matter over from every angle. He talked about the party and its inner workings. Despite all the convulsions it had gone through, it remained the frame that best reflected the dynamics of this situation. Its most recent struggle was one form of this reality's embodiment. Moukhtar told us about Faqih Basri and Mehdi Ben Barka and about their early, no, prescient feelings about all the contradictions the party's structure bears. Moukhtar was speaking confidently when he slipped into the particulars of the two men's personal lives. He had our full attention. This Moukhtar never went to school. He was a peasant. But he was educated in the school of the national movement that had provided an opportunity for him to register in the party on the political level. His self-confidence, fashioned by specific convictions, was his effective protection against deterioration and eventual death. Thus, I saw Moukhtar as an extremely mature man. He placed his psyche in his hand and turned it over in his fingers. He was also able to define and sketch it out, identifying spots of strength and weakness in it as well.

I saw the cat walk into the corridor. It rubbed itself against the wall. I noticed it still had some henna on its tail. The cat was pure white, unlike most cats which are spotted with black and grey. Ever since we came to the central prison, these cats have become a part of the backdrop here. Us, the cats, the guards, and the bars.

When we decided to paint or whitewash our cells, we asked Moha what color paint he wanted Oum Khalid to bring. We put him in charge of it. All we wanted was to ease his suffering, which was all our suffering, too. But as soon as you looked at Moha you knew how deep his pain was. Moha refused to paint his cell, saying to us mockingly,

"Is it my father's home that I should paint it?"

"It's *your* home. *Your* home, Moha. Twenty years. Who would believe it? Easy to say the words 'twenty years,' but who would believe it?"

Salah said this without paying attention to how his words would affect Moha who slinked off. But four days after we talked with him about it, he asked me to tell Lalla Aicha to bring him some henna if she could. We didn't ask him what he wanted the henna for. We just conveyed his request to her. As much as it surprised me, I justified it knowing how much Moha was suffering. It might have been an itch for which the henna would be an effective treatment. But when she brought it the following week and Moha opened the package, his face lit up when he saw it. He sniffed it, thanked Lalla Aicha, and took off. To our surprise, the next day the cat's white tail had been hennaed. Moha amused himself all the time with that cat. He stroked its back. He gently grabbed its tail. And he laughed as he concentrated on painting its tail with henna as it stood on its hind legs. Whenever the henna rubbed off, Moha would reapply it. What he wanted was for the earthiness of the henna's colors to come all the way here, to appear in front of him in any form.

Moukhtar got up to say goodbye to Leila and me. We went with him to the end of the corridor where he slipped out into the yard, and from there, to the entrance leading to death row. We followed him with our eyes without realizing how drawn we were to the man until he disappeared from view. Then we turned to one another, seizing what remained of the time.

Leila asked me how Salah was doing and asked me to call him over if I could. We no longer saw Salah in the corridor except for on days when his son and some members of his family came to visit. Before, you'd find Salah joining in with everyone else welcoming the families, every day of the week. If Rabia came to visit Abid on the same day as his mother, you'd find Salah talking with her, discussing what was happening on the outside. And when Abid would turn to his mother, Salah would ask Rabia questions about everything under the sun. Salah was where all visits came together. But now, he was satisfied going out for visits that were just for him, the most precious of those being when his son, Samad, came. Salah was liberal with everything: exercise, the library, the TV room, and even with pigeons that reproduced to no end. He was liberal with everything. Who would have thought that one day Salah would give up a flock of pigeons, and Bilqis, the pigeon that taught him all the flirtatious arts? That's what he had named it that first week as it strutted about in front of him. It had been given to Rachid El Omri on his birthday. We didn't know how Rachid had gotten it, but Salah was the first one to head to his cell to wish him a happy birthday, and Rachid insisted he take it, since he seemed so dazzled by it.

"My God! A pigeon in a cell. That's fantastic!"

That's what Salah said, and that's how Bilqis became his. He would always tell his family that when they visited, they should mention the pigeons. And Salah attended to their mating and propagation. The pigeons multiplied, presenting the basic problem of what to feed them. How could we have the resources for pigeons? We laughed loudly as Salah, right then, added this point to the agenda of tasks for one of the committees. And that is how the pigeons that had been given up by Salah would turn into one of our food resources, after we had been trying to find a food source for them!

When Leila insisted on seeing Salah, I commented,

"First Moukhtar, then Salah! Who next?"

"Don't worry. There's only half an hour left before the end of the visit."

When I said this, I was hoping to encourage her to back down, not because I didn't want Salah to take up what time was left of Leila's visit. Rather, I didn't want to have to try and convince him to go out to see her. Leila didn't know that more than ever before, Salah was dragging around tails of sadness these days. I couldn't understand in any tangible way why he was so sad. There were so many things here in prison that a person could not grasp or assimilate. A shiver of joy might flow through your body and seep into your entire being, and then suddenly, your joy is transformed into sadness without you knowing why. Of course, we knew that being here in the prison darkness was enough to explain these transformations and mood swings. And after Moha's suicide, we started to be haunted by a fear of death such as we had not experienced since we got here. Samad Mehdaoui, was different. He was martyred in the hospital, far from view.

What happened with Moha was decisive and enough to push the Laoulabi group to present three copies of a letter to the authorities requesting that they issue a pardon on their behalf, and which included a self-critique and renunciation of the entire experience. This amounted to an announcement of their total repentance. The Ministry of the Interior would not let the event pass without applauding it. So, it sent a photocopy of the letter to the news agency which subsequently distributed excerpts that transmitted news of the letter to all the newspapers. Then after that, it transmitted the entire letter. We were surprised by its tenor and contents. Only right then did I understand the mystery of Salah's sadness. I didn't understand what he had meant by something he said to Leila when she asked him to come out and insisted on seeing him. He surprised me by accepting and rushed out to her in the corridor. They embraced warmly and we sat down, chatting about all sorts of things. Then Salah alluded to the fact that what was to come would be more difficult than what had already passed.

13

THE NEWSPAPERS MADE THEIR WAY to us, and the news spread as quick as lightning. The Laoulabi group did not think the letter, considered by the Ministry of the Interior to be a consensus document, would be distributed so widely both nationally and internationally, especially after they had included such nonsense in it. Laoulabi and his group had wanted things to remain limited to a demand for pardons. They would wait for that demand to be met which would result in their release from prison. But things took another turn. When we read the document in its official wording, we did not find a self-critique pointing to particular people and their relationship to a specific experience. Rather, it was an attack on our characters prior to the experience. Distortion, shaming, and slander hung from the ink on the page. It was awful. There was no way this could have come from one of us! What we were reading was much worse than what the Makhzen said when it caught us in its web of accusations. Salah knew that the group was engaging in an assessment plan, even though of all the groups, this one's individual members most strongly rejected any type of assessment. In fact, until now, a group assessment of the experience had not been done because of them. They took advantage of Salah's vulnerable state and presented the project to him. They demanded that he agree to sign a letter he hadn't seen. We didn't know that until the letter fell into our hands. We were furious. We yelled and cursed as we never had before.

We wanted to light them all on fire. Laoulabi came out with his group and headed straight to the prison administration. It was shameful. They asked the administration for protection against us. This was the icing on the cake. We walked back to the yard, and *they* remained out in front of the administration for more than half an hour. After that they slinked off one by one to their cells and closed their doors on the recommendation of the administration. We traded insults which only ceased when we heard heart-rending sounds coming from Salah. He added tears of grief as he counted on his fingers.

"After fifteen years. After one hundred and eighty months. After Samad Mehdaoui's martyrdom and losing Moha. After our defeat and us coming apart and our souls having been flayed. After losing those we loved and those we would have loved. After planting something akin to life in the basements of our tombs, because cells are no different than tombs. They threw us into cells, completely and utterly exhausted, with the toilet right there at our feet. This is where we sleep, and this is where we wake up. This is where we piss, and this is where we shit. For years. This is where everything is. It's no wider than your outstretched hands, if you tuck them in a bit. And it's as long as your body, shorter actually, since the toilet blocks your feet. Still, we made this grave into a place, and we shined here after they threw us in with the intent to kill us. We shined here in spite of ourselves, and Laoulabi comes along with his group to snuff us out like this.

"After all is said and done, *this* is how we're humiliated. If only it had been our choice. Look carefully with me at all these losses and look closely at how we've been betrayed today!"

Salah gasped as he said all this. I feared for him as I never had before. He was counting off the years in prison and converting them into months and days, and as he enumerated everything, he wept louder. Salah wept hard: all those years being arranged as a never-ending series of numbers. Laoulabi and his group's letter was enough to restore much of the unity that had been shattered among the rest of the groups. We began to greet one another and sit together in the yard, even exchanging news that had arrived from the outside after we had stopped doing this. We were united, but only against the insult caused by the Laoulabi group, which had turned into a "mangy camel" (as the ancient poet, Tarafa, put it) that didn't come out to the yard anymore or meet us in the corridor. They would just move in and out of their cells all day. Even their visits to one another started to dwindle as well. They started to spend most of their time cooped up inside their cells, especially when their letter was ignored and their pardon denied. In fact, not only did they come to avoid running into *us*, but they came to run away from one another as well.

It was a wonderful day when Samad Mehdaoui's wife came to visit us. It was the first time Kenza's feet had crossed the central prison's threshold because Samad had died right before we had demanded in-person visits (along with all the other demands we made at the time). We crowded around Kenza and asked her how things were going with her and about the health of her two children, Nada and Samad. When we were detained, Samad Mehdaoui had left Kenza two months' pregnant with her second child. And when she gave birth, we were still languishing somewhere in dark police stations and secret detention centers. In fact, many families had already begun to prepare for news of our permanent disappearances. That's why Kenza named the baby after his father who, at the time, was still counted among the missing. And when we appeared in court, Samad learned that his child, now two years old, was coming. He asked what his name was, and they said they hadn't named him yet. He encouraged them to name him Ghassan. He urged Kenza as he looked down, avoiding her eyes. He looked at her neck and her chest, then he raised his gaze up to her hair. The important thing was for him to try not to see the sadness that had settled in her eyes, a sadness that was his fault. Kenza, who only knew about school, ballet, and playing piano.

For Samad to get involved with her that afternoon and for her to head, every day, to the college to see him without understanding the meaning of his political activities that took place outside the small number of classes he didn't even have time to attend. The first thing Kenza did for him when she walked up to the door of the government office was to add his name to that of her son's. There was nothing to stop her from doing so at the Civil Status Department where one of her relatives worked. But, since it was a matter that had to do with a martyr, every obstacle was placed before her. And that despite the fact that the entire family started to call Ghassan by Samad's name, except for Kenza, who continued to call him by his full name. That's how she told us about Ghassan Samad Mehdaoui, who was growing up.

"He looks a lot like Samad. He's sixteen years old now. He does well in school. I talk a lot with him about his father and about you all. Every time I come, he insists on visiting you, but I'm putting that off until he's grown, and grown some more . . ."

"No, no. How can he grow up while we're in here?! Tell him we'll visit him at home," quipped Salah.

Kenza let out a laugh that diffused its sweet aroma all through the corridor. We hovered around Kenza. She asked us about Laoulabi and his group and confirmed that she was here to see all of us, that she knew us as people and comrades of the martyr, her husband, Samad, and that there was no connection between her and our differences.

"I am here to sniff Samad's scent too, so send Laoulabi and the rest of our friends."

"Kenza, Laoulabi has no color. He has no smell. In fact, his stench makes our noses run. God forbid he have any of Samad's smell on him . . ."

Kenza stared at Abid who gesticulated wildly as he spoke. She insisted again that we go get the Laoulabi group, so each one of us urged the other to undertake this mother of all tasks.

We tried to convince Salah to take it on because he could formulate the call in poetry.

"God forbid I sully my poetry with the name of Laoulabi and his group!"

Kenza looked pleadingly at Salah, and he dragged himself heavily toward the entrance of the cell block. We didn't know what he said to them, but we looked over from Kenza to see them coming toward us, heads bowed. Laoulabi entwined his fingers then undid them and put his hands into his pants pockets. They walked toward us looking embarrassed, as if they had been caught red-handed. Kenza got up and walked toward them and began to hug them all.

Kenza was a woman in every meaning of the word, even though it is extremely difficult to know exactly what that means. I could see this without being able to fully understand it. Kenza left that evening like a refreshing breeze. Her strong presence remained with us and we held onto it and discussed it all week.

But is this how a martyr's wife should be? How could we burden Kenza with the task of preserving the martyr's name? What did Kenza have to do with all of this? Where did Kenza fit in to all this suffering and need? When Samad Mehdaoui was martyred, Kenza was no more than twenty-four years old. Now, after all this time, could we let the martyr's wife go? We accept our women and our girlfriends as colorful decorations, as a low-cut back in a tight-fitting dress, as a bit of red on the lips. But with Kenza, the martyr's wife, we didn't all *have to* agree on hanging a sign on her forehead that said she was public property. Thus, we burdened this woman with the cost of bearing witness and of martyrdom to preserve the name of the martyr, as if we were actually setting her free and allowing her to blossom. That for her to live her life was to touch that inheritance that we placed on her shoulders without asking her whether it was too heavy. All we liberally granted her was a mist of nonsense; ways to commemorate the martyr. What was Kenza's place in all of this? Did we ask her what it was that she had lost, and what it was she was still losing? Why did we insist on running so fast inside the cage? Those who killed Samad didn't plan for half a lifetime for that, yet we insist on starving for an *entire* lifetime. Why didn't we insist on seeing Kenza in something other than mourning clothes?

I was starting to think that we asked a lot of our women. When she came to visit, I looked at Leila, then thought of Rabia, Zina, Samira, and all the others who still put up with us and endured us being here in prison. The questions come one after the other: After we get out, if getting out is our fate, will all those bodies hanging around the alleys and streets tempt us? Will our heads turn and pay attention to all those round behinds that shake all around us? I felt a bit embarrassed asking these questions. It is a difficult thing to feel ashamed of oneself, but this is what happened when I gazed at Leila, Rabia, Samira, Zina. The least we could possibly do for them was to save them a place that grows, not only in our hearts, minds, and veins, but also in our eyes. I have to see with my eyes that have only Leila in them. I insisted on this despite the resounding echo of so many comrades' relationships that had broken up when they got out before us, after completing their ten-year sentences. I knew that some relationships exploded immediately after a month or two, like those of Ismail, Rajae, Fouad, and Nouzha. The only thing that could not be handed a sentence or even understood was the relationship between two people, between a man and a woman. How does it start? How does it deepen? And how does it end? Leila said that the ex-prisoner is more devoted to life than any other creature.

"You all ravenously consume life and all its trappings. The detainee feels a double-loss and that same detainee hopes for double-compensation when he gets to grab on once again to the outside, to life. That's how you gluttonous demons were raised. You gobble up sex, bread, wine, the ocean. You even wolf down the smell of dirt!"

I stared at Leila as she enumerated the list of appetites, providing explanatory details with the contours of her face and her gesturing hands. I grabbed them close to me and said,

"But you know that the detainee's voracious appetite for sex is an impossible issue. Prison has destroyed us and restoration won't be easy."

Leila burst out laughing, immediately commenting,

"Why? Is there injury, God forbid?"

I knew that Leila was aware of our problems and our sufferings in detail, our sexual deprivation, the complications of our sex life (if we were having sex at all). But what I didn't know was how unabashedly sarcastic she could be when discussing our torment. I didn't have a chance to ask her to explain. Leila's tone quickly changed, and I knew that her justification for certain things was just idle talk, no more, no less. She exploded into bitterness as she spoke about Nouzha and how serious things had gotten when Ismail decided to end their relationship after she had waited for ten years while he served his sentence here in the central prison.

"You know what? No one mentions sacrifice and stepping up anymore. Time has started to form new values. Nouzha needs to forget everything that happened before. In fact, she needs to close the door on it."

Everyone could see that Ismail had gone too far with all his scheming and shouting. Nouzha told that to Souad, Leila, and Rabia. She cried until she collapsed. She bent over his hands and kissed them. But Ismail wasn't there. Women are strong on more than one level. They plunge headlong into more than one area and absorb more than one task. But when it has anything to do with the body, they are destroyed with the first hesitation or jolt. Nouzha thought that if she could just bond physically with Ismail, it wouldn't be possible for their relationship to fade. She held onto it with her teeth. She said that she went as far as she could in this relationship. If you asked her what she meant by "as far as she could," she would allude to

the sexual. If only Nouzha had recognized before that her pre-
dicament was woven into the very fabric of women's history,
she might have slipped from its clutches. What was sex compared to Nouzha making her way to the central prison for ten
years? What did sex mean when Nouzha faithfully made the
journey winter and summer? What did it mean when someone
turned right and left and found that they have lost ten years of
their life? What does it mean, and what does it mean?!

Rajae was the complete opposite of Nouzha. As soon as
she felt that the relationship had started to become a burden,
she screamed and woke up. Rajae only saw Fouad occasion-
ally now. Fouad, Ismail, and the group that was released with
them went off in another direction. They started to establish a
political framework, by-laws, general features, and foundation
which they had tried to form here inside the prison. A year
after they got out, they began to publish a weekly newspaper
that paved the way for their political project, even though their
focus was on the cultural (at this stage of development, this
made the framework appear to be primarily a cultural project). All those who carried the project had previously adhered
to the experience of the two halves of the Left, and that which
was contained within the organization. This forced them to
open a discussion with Abdelrahman Saâdi (a national figure
living in exile) for him to head up the organization's project
and serve as the bridge between young people's experiences
and the historical roots of the national movement. It was
mandatory—and mutual agreement on it was implicit—to
bet on the relationship with the masses and their memories
of Abdelkrim el-Khattabi, Ahmed el-Hansali, Hoummane
Fetouaki, and Brahim Roudani which still burned bright.
The project was taken up by young people, all of whom were
distinguished by their Marxist leftist experience which could
not be officially tolerated, or at least stated publicly. Although
memory was ignited by national heritage, I saw it as a current
memory that could only be conditioned on the present and

the future. Foaud Khashli was up to his ears in the project, and Rajae was there, still waiting for a time slot on the weekend. But Fouad, like all those delusions, never arrived. Rajae continued to wait, then she woke up, which she told us during a visit. Rajae had decided to separate from Fouad. We tried to calm her down, but she erupted like a volcano, followed by a whisper. She talked and she wept, her tears falling down her neck. She just let them flow without wiping them away, just like she let her words flow from her mouth all on their own.

"Believe me, I really tried putting off this decision, thinking that Fouad might pay attention to the fractures that caused my heart to bleed, but he wasn't there. I'm not asking him to neglect what he has made a priority, but I don't accept, I *will* not accept coming second to last on his list of concerns. I've been waiting here for ten years, and even now, I'm still waiting for a man who only shows up at dawn. Should I wait another ten years? I'm not waiting anymore for someone to emerge out from the prison's darkness. Now I'm there by the window, behind the door waiting to hear the sound of his footsteps, the roar of a car engine. I'm waiting for the end of that last meeting when the multitudes will cast him out while I lean on my wounds, cursing a woman who happens to be me, no different than any other woman waiting for her drunk or unruly husband when the last of the bars has thrown him out after dawn. Don't tell me there's no comparison. We've waited enough. I'm just listening to my heart is all."

Rajae talks and cries. We all felt her pain. Rabia and Leila, who had come to visit us, sat close to her, and listened. They were stupefied. Rabia moved closer to Rajae to wipe her tears away. A silence began to settle over our heads in the corridor. The only sounds were Rajae's broken sobs. Us men don't cling stubbornly to women only at the beginning of the relationship. Especially when it isn't a normal or easy relationship, or when we feel them pulling away as we start to lose them, and it is within their power to stop the course of a given relationship.

Only then do we wake up and say to them, "You are *mine* and mine only. After me, there's nothing else!"

Rajae's decision was a violent blow to Fouad Khashli's emotional life. He only woke up and came to his senses after Rajae had already made up her mind. He tried to repair all the cracks, but Rajae had already left.

Part Two

Good evening, my wounds

14

GOOD EVENING, MY DEAR WOUNDS. Tali' al-'Urayfi has decided to exhume you, and I would not refuse Tali' a request. Tali' is a man who comes from a page in an Abdul Rahman Munif novel. Now I am like someone being shoved from behind to tell about what I saw through the intense blackness of the blindfold for half a day coupled with the madness of night. Tali' urged me to talk about the details of those days in the secret police station. But I am not the same Shahrazad who covers over the mad pitch blackness of night with stories. I gather my scattered strength, and while I whisper in al-'Urayfi's ear about stories of transparent wounds—wounds you can see through—he scrutinizes me and says,

"Sit here, Leila, with your heart at ease. Sit here, and your beauty, the freshness of your wound will bandage my own."

Here I am now, sitting in the corner of sadness like a tear in the middle of the night. How can Tali' bandage my wound while he himself is covered in wounds? I thought talking about it would require a lot of time to gather and organize my memories, but Tali' urged me just to narrate the fragments. Anyone who reads this pain and carries a piece of us with them can rearrange the pages. Tali' brought me around to this opinion. How can I hold back, overcome, feel the burning of the whip and the electricity, then bear the burden of organizing all of this for you so you can lean back in bed, or put one leg over the other in a café, and read my pain?! . . . I carry a piece of

Tali' al-'Urayfi inside me. Tali' who exploded there. He wears me down here. He destroys me and reignites all the questions I have. I stopped short of telling all the details. I loved this al-'Urayfi who clad himself in lines and letters to stand broad and tall like a towering tree. In him I remembered Haidar's novel *A Banquet for Seaweed* and how the prose reads like poetry. *A Banquet for Seaweed* dazzles me when it claims that death, killing, and torture are the most beautiful things one can express, their power concealed when the poetic self extends from the top of the text until just before the end. I find myself in the highest state of mysticism with Fulla Bouanab's powerful story and with Mahdi Jawad, the story's narrator. The despotic character 'Ubayd Allah al-Kulaybi stopped me in my tracks. A character torn from the banner of the rising national tide to be reincarnated as the embodiment of condescending oppression. I recall how my heart went back and forth during the war. At that moment, I was prepared to sacrifice myself, not for al-Kulaybi, not even for the people. But rather, solely for the Arab glass that was shattering inside of me. Now, as I gather up the details of al-Kulaybi's brutality in Haidar's *Banquet*, I feel a nausea just like the nausea I felt in July. Don't tell me, Tali', "Start from here, from the nausea," because I don't know why I'm still putting off telling the story. Perhaps to singe some of those watchful guardians—my father, my brother, some of those writers—while you remain, the one and only to all my fire, to burn even more by providing the fuel. No! I will start from here, a state of extreme mysticism with my body. He scrutinizes it, sinking his eyes onto the curves of my breast, trembling, saying, and I quote,

"I swear, if they asked what the greatest thing in existence was, I'd say it was a woman's breast."

I was on the verge of tears, about to sob as I never had before. A lump lodged in my throat that burned my heart. My tears started to flow but I pushed them back. My appetite shrank to almost nothing. Oh, God, why do the beloved and the interrogator become one in their attraction to and love of breasts? I recalled those July days in the secret prison. I recalled them in all their intensity. I was a dead body seeking mercy in Father Yiannaros's monastery. My heart beat so hard it might have been torn from its place or stopped beating altogether. Fear is something fundamental in us, and I don't trust anyone who talks about a mute steadfastness that exists in the prisons of this country. Why should we turn *their* brutality into our virtuous steadfastness? Why should we reduce the size of everything they do to us and explain it away as natural? I hadn't yet come to terms with my body when they had me strip naked.

"Take everything off, or else we'll do it for you."

I felt my bra underneath my sweater, and when I went to take off my jeans, I touched my panties just to check what underwear I was wearing. I was scared and ashamed to appear in front of them in the skimpy ones that looked like a *baghrir* pancake, the ones that Farida had given me as a gift just two weeks before my detention. I relaxed a little when I could feel that it was made of thicker cloth, meaning it covered me up somewhat. Imagine, Tali', how a pair of panties can become a shield against the interrogators. I hadn't rid myself of the fear when I became overcome with anguish. With anything having to do with my body, I was still a little girl wrapped in shyness. When I started to take off my pants, I had given up trying to remove the bra. I reached behind my back to open the clasp. I tried, but it was no use. I couldn't get my hands behind my back, perhaps because of how much they were shaking. They walked toward me and pulled at it from the front. It stretched in their hands. Then they beat me hard on my chest. The first thing that caught the interrogators' attention as I stood there in nothing but my panties was my breasts, or rather, my nipples. I could feel them winking at one another, despite the thick blindfold over my eyes. Their words gave them away. They laughed out loud and walked toward me. One of them began to pull at my nipple (I thought of the poet, Nizar Qabbani, and how he constructed monumental pyramids out of nipples) while another one screamed at me, spittle hitting me in my face,

"The socialist sons of bitches are experts with girls! Look at this perfect body, and she says she's in politics!"

It was then that I was sure I wasn't in the grips of some gang that was just passing through. Rather, I was with the *Mukhabarat*, the intelligence police. Despite that, I was still betting that there had been some sort of mistake. I hadn't yet crossed the threshold of the party and become a member. Whenever the idea of joining the organization was suggested to me, I felt suffocated, which caused me to stop attending the sympathizers' discussion circles, and . . .

But why did the agents focus on snapping profanities at us from the start? Because the words they attributed to me were what again made me feel that something suspicious was going on. I remained hopeful. Rather, I pushed hope to its extreme and imagined that they were just going to ask me my name, then apologize and let me go.

They left, slamming the door behind them. Four hours later by my confused estimate, they rushed back into the room intent on something. Whatever it was, I didn't know. My heart began to race. When we were young, we always repeated something like "the teacher hit me until I saw stars." And this wasn't just nonsense either. The blindfold was still tied over my eyes when I saw the star go by. Yes, I saw it after the first slap, then with the barrage of slaps that followed. But stars in police stations don't shine. The worst thing is when you're slapped without being able to sense that the one slapping you is winding up; when you're completely surprised by the slap, not being able to see the hand come down on your face which might allow you to move your head back a little to absorb the blow. Then, they moved on to the whipping session that began to work its way up to tracing its virility on my body. Nausea creeps up my throat. Acid drops onto my heart. I don't remember how I fell to the floor, nor how I woke up to a new body-coloring session. But why did the interrogators focus on slapping our left cheek and applying electricity to the left nipple? I thought that maybe it was their way of extracting the "no" they thought resided only on the left side of the body. Moving on to the second session made the first one seem like little more than a warmup. I was chopped into little pieces of pain when they stretched my body. My head down below and my legs hung up high in the air like a pair of pants hanging upside down from a clothesline. I felt the pain increase in every part of my body, a burning in my back, a tingling all over. I didn't know the source of the water dripping onto my body, my belly, my chest, my neck, then my face. Was it coming from the room's damp ceiling, or was there someone holding his breath here, close to me in the room, who specialized in tormenting me with these intermittent drops that walk like ants or like flowing salt over my body? All I wanted was for them to untie me and let me scratch myself. Then, my body fell with a thud. I imagined my broken body parts falling to the floor. All of a sudden, the door was pushed open. I was in excruciating pain. I was writhing in pain and still feeling nauseous. Even though the door was open, I didn't sense footsteps coming toward me. After a few minutes, a bunch of agents rushed in. Their boisterous laughter got louder in fits and starts. Their shouting reached my ear.

"Whadda you need, naked ass?"

That's what they said. And before they were done shouting, they ordered the Hadj to hand me my clothes after they had lowered me down to the ground and left. My questioning hadn't even begun yet, not to mention my interrogation. And I was still hoping that there had been some sort of mistake.

After the Hadj removed what remained of the ties and undid the blindfold, he slinked off to get my clothes. I rubbed my eyes. The fog stretched out in front of me. Little by little, the indistinct shape of the Hadj—that's what they called him—began to fade away, to disappear completely, before I had a chance to get a good look at him. My sight started to return. The room looked square. Empty except for a metal bed thrown there in a corner. Here on my right, a locked door, and beyond that, the door of the room my cell was in. I looked closely at my belly. I lowered my eyes a bit more. I examined myself and broke out crying. My chest, my legs, my whole body were splattered with blood. But the blood wasn't from the whip. It was menstrual blood. I had started to flow early. I stretched my hand up to my neck and face, peeling off bits of dried blood. I put my head in my hands and burst out crying. I cried harder than I ever had before. These weren't drops of water that had fallen from the ceiling onto me. No. They were drops of blood. *My* blood. Hearing me wail, the guard hurried in. He looked at me a bit and picked me up so I could go to the water closet, which was behind the door I had seen to my right. He stopped me there and rushed to bring me a small piece of cloth. As soon as I set foot inside, the cockroaches living there in the corners climbed up the walls, causing some flakes of gypsum to fall onto the toilet seat. I hurried over to the seat and sat down. I turned the tap on. The water was cold. I peed. I washed myself gently. I picked flecks of blood off my vagina. I wiped myself with the piece of cloth that I realized was a sock. It smelled awful. I looked closely at it. I tossed it into the water container, but it just floated around on the surface. I turned off the tap and went out. I took off my underpants. I folded them four times after tucking the wet part underneath and stuck them inside my pants to absorb the rest of the flowing blood. As soon as I was done, the Hadj came. He put the blindfold back on and took me by the hand to where I had been before. I lowered my body like a weight. I sat in that room and scratched my leg. I put my hand on the wall. I thought about Abbas who had passed through here. Perhaps he had been here in the same room. But when his face peered at me here, I remembered his aspirations for a society of tomorrow as he pointed to the biggest hotel in the city, specifically to its extensive gardens, and said, "In the society of tomorrow, we'll turn this hotel into the educational committee's headquarters." He pointed to the gardens as he said, "This is where the children will find enough space for big games." I bumped into the wall and knew that I had reached the edge of the room. I went back to where I started and decided to measure the room and memorize the dimensions for Abbas so we could, in the society of tomorrow, search for this room and decide what we would use it for. It measured no larger than five meters wide and six meters long. With his innocent face and his pure childlike laugh, Abbas scratched in the dirt to lift the society of tomorrow up from below, like a child inflating the tires of his small toy bike for them to get bigger and bigger and run over the guards' tanks. I felt blood coming out of me to which I had nothing to add except for my bra which I had made into a belt to prevent some of the pain in my belly. I folded it twice, made sure the clasp was in back and stuck *it* into my pants. Trust me, Tali', we might hear about the electric charge, and about the "airplane" (even if we'd never dreamt of flying in it, a free-ride. No visas or passports are required inside police stations). We also get to know the different types of whips. How long they are. How thick they are. What kind they are. We become familiar with bottles and how they threaten to break all breakable hymens. I don't know why they only threaten us with Coca Cola bottles. When they call the bottles by name, Sonallah Ibrahim comes to mind, and I think to myself, here's yet another use for Coca Cola. Yes, we can envision all that, Tali', but other forms of torture don't immediately come to mind. We don't read about them in books or hear about others experiencing them. Things one should prepare for. Imagine me at home, in bed, in my pajamas, with hot milk mixed with cinnamon. I have everything I need. These are the necessary monthly rituals—at my mother's, alone, with Mohammed. And then for me to find myself hung upside down, then thrown on the floor with the whip tracing lines of blood all over my body, blood from inside me. When I realized that I was menstruating, I cried so hard because I had forgotten about it. I forgot to forget that I was a woman. I cried harder than I had ever cried before. When they brought the whip down on my body, I was tough, I faced it. But the moment I started menstruating, it made me feel an essential weakness that caused me to break down and cry. How could I overcome this? You, Tali', can talk about what you've seen them do to a woman named Salwa. You can describe what happened to Salwa. But to take possession of every detail of Salwa's voice, you need to *be* Salwa. All of us, us women and you men, share the whip, electricity, and being torn apart. But, my dear Tali', we do not share menstrual blood.

Naked. Covered in blood. When the thought of the Lebanese painter, Guiragossian struck me, I was still sobbing as he moved toward me. He plunged his brush into the colors and skillfully painted the canvas. This Guiragossian looms large from one painting to another. I wouldn't know anything about him if my friend, Nabil Qozah, hadn't brought pictures of his paintings from Lebanon. I immediately wondered if my voracious love of them was because practically all the bodies, their lower halves anyway, their legs, were longer than the upper parts, the chests, and heads. But, as I looked at more and more paintings, they seemed to reveal what I really loved about them. Yes! It was that the bodies needed to be stretched out for their lower parts to be planted deeply into the earth. This Guiragossian, from the other side of the sea, whose paintings I loved, towers above the rest. He stabs his brush into the heart's blood and produces tall naked bodies, stretched along a road we have never walked, sprawling like Beirut's sorrow, a warm fountain like the heat of purpose we still stumble over in his paintings. With his brush, Guiragossian practices a humane type of violence against the savagery of humankind. Before the savagery of the interrogators tears the clothing from our bodies, Guiragossian's brush rushes to remove us from it with impressionistic gentleness. Yes, Guiragossian is humane violence pitted against the savagery of humankind.

Saadia also came to mind. The brown-skinned girl from the south whose family was inherited by my grandmother's family. Her relatives worked for us in various cities. Once, Jamila, Hayat, and I were preparing for the Baccalaureate exam when Saadia came in with a tray of tea. We asked her to sit with us and she did. Conversation moved to Hayat telling us about the pain and cramps she gets when she menstruates, specifically at the end of the second week of the month, meaning the fourteenth day. Jamila said that her discomfort took the form of a migraine and sharp pains in the back of her head and in the forehead, usually coming between the twenty-sixth and twenty-eighth days of every month. So, their periods were regular. Saadia couldn't bear remaining silent about a topic she knew well and she insisted on diving in with her thoughts too. She told us that she didn't suffer from cramps, and that this heavy visitor came calling between the thirty-sixth and fortieth days of each month. We burst out laughing as we tried to come up with a month that consisted of thirty-six days. While we rolled around laughing, Saadia swore it was a special day in her menstrual cycle. That's how Saadia was. Insistent. That it was a goat even if it flew. And that's how a thirty-six day month was added to our calendar. Whenever we met in the high school foyer, we'd burst out laughing.

Saadia didn't know how to read or write, but she had an uncanny ability for devouring an enormous number of words in formal Arabic, whether from news broadcasts and advertisements or from discussions among us as we prepared for our exams. Shortly after she came to our house, Saadia learned about Taha Hussein, 'Abbas Mahmoud al-'Aqqad, and Badr Shakir al-Sayyib. She learned that Brazil was a country that exports *bunn*, or coffee beans, which is another word for *qahwa*, or coffee. One day when she handed me a letter the postman had delivered, I thanked her, and she responded with the first Arabic phrase that came to mind. She answered coquettishly and playfully, using the standard Moroccan response,

"No need to thank me."

"Better to respond using the more formal 'but of course.' It's more concise. Better and simpler than what you said," I replied.

"But I wanna answer in Arabic, not French!"

That is how "but of course" would remain a French phrase in Saadia's lexicon. And thus, whenever I retreated into my blood-filled body, the memories extended outward as a window from which I must look—despite the shaking and bad timing—at something that's still worthy of attention. Here, in the deepest reaches of my heart, I sometimes smiled about things that seemed mundane, sometimes silly too. And I am overwhelmed with crying about unfunny things. But the window I opened this time onto my memories of that period of detention was a window wrapped in pain that would only open just enough for my head to fit through. Tali' said to me, "Thread the two periods of time together and talk about them as if they were one event." No, Tali', this time the event was clothed in more than one robe. They excelled at it this time. They didn't heap profanities on me. Not at all. In fact, there was no time for talk. They moved directly to the application, to choking me with questions that went beyond anything that had to do with Moukhtar's case. The nausea this time was incredible. They put me down on my knees and ordered me to stick out my hand and grab onto something. I felt it, flaccid in front of me. As soon as I realized what it was, I wanted to puke my guts out. Yes, I was sick to my stomach just because I had placed my hand on one of their penises. It was splattered with sticky liquid. I tried to pull my hand back, but they kicked me, and I fell on my face, only for them to pull me up. But when I refused to stick my hand out again, they pushed me back down on my knees and one of them rubbed his penis over my neck and face. I puked. I felt twice as ashamed as when they had pounded on my ribs and body. Now I call to mind *your* experience, Tali'. I call to mind my digging into Moukhtar's case. I call to mind Mouline and his comrades' cases as they sat in the darkness of the central prison. I call all of this to mind. I think about it for a while. And it seems insignificant, small in comparison to the size of what horrible wickedness they did to us. Because as a result of digging into Moukhtar's case, I became someone who was colluding with foreigners against state security. The accusation weighed more than I did (having lost a lot of weight, settling in at fifty-two kilos! It was like pitting an ant against an accusation the size of an elephant). The accusation was much larger than me. I couldn't even easily say it. I defended myself. I clarified my background research into the case. I yelled as loudly as I could, but their whip was the master. Until now, I had not yet grasped why they did not present me directly at trial. The case was filled to the brim with tons of accusations that had been prepared and typed up. Whenever they dragged me, blindfolded, to the interrogation room, whenever I heard them turn the machine on after each question (something that didn't happen when I was detained in July), they had just three questions, all of which had to do with my position in the party and my responsibility inside the youth organization. During those days in July, I was still in a constant daze, so I wrapped myself in silence. I considered my lack of party affiliation enough of a justification to remain necessarily quiet. And when they whipped me, I remained silent. During those days in July, they did not interrogate me for more than two sessions, dedicating the rest of the time I was in their care to whipping, flaying, and terrorizing me. And now they were stitching the charges into a pack saddle they would ride on my back.

After that, I learned that the administrative staff that was there when I visited Moukhtar had been completely dispersed.

Their punishment was for them to be placed in different prisons of the south (and you have no idea about the prisons of the south!) in order to guard those who had been forcibly kidnapped. They were considered to have been complicit with me in facilitating my visit with Moukhtar. Of course, the guard who was in charge of registration at the main entrance to the prison made me feel ashamed about it day and night. What did it mean for someone in the country's center to be sent to its margins without any prior warning? It became clear that Moukhtar's case was known by the international community when it was included in one of Amnesty International's reports. It was clear that the news item cited the conversation I had had with him inside Gharbia. Of course, the issue cut two ways. One part of it was their clumsiness in presenting me at trial with a direct accusation having to do with my conversation with Moukhtar, at least in the interim. They might soon be searching for something else far from the hoopla that they could try me on that might serve as provocation if a link were made with the case. It wasn't certain, but rather a mere possibility that I began to put together after the period of my secret detention had exceeded forty days, with neither trial nor release on the horizon.

The last time I visited Zahra, I noticed that she was anxious and tense. I didn't know why. I simply attributed it to fatigue and exhaustion. At the end of the visit, I said goodbye as the corridor spit me out into the courtyard. I saw the guards' eyes fall onto me, so I made my way quickly toward the main entrance. There, two agents grabbed me, one on my right where he put his hand under my arm, while the other agent's hands remained slack, even though he remained very much in contact with my body. What was going on? The two men were extremely good at pretending to know me well. It didn't awaken the curiosity of that band still waiting with their baskets in front of the prison gate. We took less than four steps to where an R4—a Renault 4, that "makes you feel safe," as the commercials tell you day and night in its ad campaign comprised of nonsense made to convince us how safe they were to ride in—was waiting for us. But when you're stuck between two agents, all you feel in that car is utter ruin. One of the agents pushed me in to sit down between them in the back seat. The other grabbed me and shoved my head forward.

"Watch your head," he said as the other put the blindfold over my eyes. The car started up and sped down the road with the agent on my right giving directions.

"Take Bouya Omar Road."

All I still remember about them is how much this clutch of agents looked alike, as if they were one man. Why do all agents look the same? They weren't yellow or white. Nor did they tend toward dark-skinned. I tried to determine their color from the delicate position I was in with my head still pushed down. Leaning my back forward like that created a tingling sensation at the top of my neck and in my waist. But all I could remember of their faces was how filthy they were. They were the color of filth. Every agent is filthy until proven guilty, sorry, I mean proven *innocent*, because guilt's counterpart, innocence, should be the basis for proving its opposite. The R4 drove over unpaved roads for more than three hours before we arrived at the detention site headquarters. To this day, I still hate riding in R4s. This Renault 4, I don't know why I had to suffer it twice. Was this Renault 4 all they had? I thought that everyone who passed through here, through this country's secret prisons, had been driven here in this Renault 4. But Mouline, there in Gharbia, would refute that when he told me that they took him in a fancy Mercedes that turned all the neighbors' heads as it squeezed through the narrow alleyways to pull right up to his building's door. I laughed and thought to myself that women don't deserve any more from the agents than this Renault 4. Do you know, Tali', that being detained in the police station made me long to hug every woman? My mother, my sister, Oum Walid, Oum Najwa, Leila, Zohour, Naima . . . That's right, we're the ones who have no history to support us loving one another; everything we drag and leave behind is a history of harm, malice, and conspiracy. A history established in Haroun al-Rashid's dungeons, before the Battle of the Camel, reproducing itself inside us down to our hearts. Trust me, Tali', if only we were a bit more favorably inclined toward ourselves and examined some of that history's thresholds, we would realize that the game that masterfully reproduces itself in our hearts, the game that can only be mastered by pelting us with shouts, "no"s, and the forbidden . . . I only came to like my body when I was in prison. I contemplated it for a long time as it lost blood, and I loved it. For the first time I turned to my body, in all its details and intersections.

Ah! If only we loved one another enough. Things would look so different. When so many feminist activities and organizations heeded the call to create a unified women's movement to coordinate efforts and bring the different factions together I felt our sharp lack of this love and the necessity to re-establish it. Discussion went on for more than a month about forming the framework, and most of us focused on a feminist movement with a demanding militant character. At that point in time, the phase did not eke out more than two women's associations, but for ten years, they were considered mere organizations parallel to two more established political organizations. As for the rest of the parties, they were still moving back and forth between planning for the specificity of women's status and then, subsequently, working on this front. For that reason, the question of the movement was not palatable, logically speaking. As for reaching a consensus on establishing a feminist movement that would result in more militant feminist work in this country, discussion digressed from this to a debate having to do with representation. Was it political representation or a representation of feminist activities, where emotion marked most of the interventions? What excited me was that I was able to distinguish the political and party tendencies of many of the women just from the way they analyzed things, or failed to do so. But what I could not grasp was the tune of the "independents" within this initiative. The word had been emptied of a content it never had, because I didn't understand how to be independent, but I didn't really like anyone. In fact, I lined up with other independents. I felt myself to be a true independent because when I went to meetings, I didn't bring anything other than a planned schedule of work that had been laid out from the previous meeting and a self-reflection on the subject. But when I arrived at the meeting and found independents holding a single opinion and in a state of high alert, I crumpled to the ground, put my independence in the palm of my hand, and persuaded myself that the meeting had been postponed until further notice. Until independence became not only a principle or form of organized behavior for the principle, but also a space where ideas could struggle with one another, an interrogation of an opinion and a counter-opinion, a curtailing of consensus as a mechanism generated by a fundamentalism that is only searching for certainty. Here, where the glass is implanted from the top of the head down to the bottom of the feet, and nothing can budge the heavy marble slabs in the chests of those who feel so reassured, you might ask, Tali', why should I dive into the details? You don't realize the complications of these shifts. The initiative barely crept along. In fact, it shrank, and the abyss extended between us women more than ever before. Our situation in this country, Tali', is no different from the women's situation there in Harran. Of course, up until this meeting that would be the last, I was still listening to various points of view, and I found many points of agreement. But something internal always caused us to split apart in the name of the dynasty of idols. I met Amina there for the first time. I hadn't seen her for ten years, not because we didn't move in the same circles, but rather because Amina had had enough a long time ago, ever since she married Abbas and was transformed into a housewife. Suffice it to say, she had basically "shopped" for a husband. Because things at that time were only going to produce a husband of this sort. During her formal presence at the meetings in June and in her readiness to defend a certain version of things, the issue was not on the table as far as she was concerned. But her presence seemed obligatory for the purposes of political representation, and that's what was sharply reflected in the issue's absence, rather, its omission, within her party affiliation, or more correctly, her husband's party affiliation. To the extent that the discussion proceeded, it became clear to us as a feminist self that was preparing to carry this project that we were still fragmented. You will tell me that even the powers and parties that carry a project of societal change are fragmented, but the parties stand alone. Discussion didn't drain them in their relationship to the political. Rather, it was a justification for their very existence. As for the women's associations, the same discussion has been going around in circles for ten years. Why were these associations born in the womb of political frameworks? We exhausted the discussion in this circle over the course of that period, and we were, subsequently, exhausted. Of course, the result was not that we found definitive answers, but rather, an awareness that raising questions of this type was something positive and was linked from the start, and was not the temporal extension that I knew before. When the question was transformed into an obstacle to getting to work, it became necessary to widen its scope, which did not mean that it had been canceled. True, questions cannot only be put forth on this level. Rather, they need to be engaged with on multiple levels: Why not hold women's associations accountable for their connections to political parties? Why don't we push the discussion as far as it can go and proceed from the fact that they are truly organizations parallel to those parties? But the basis was the question of how capable they were of producing feminist militants who could be relied upon to push a women's movement based on specific demands, underlining the fact that the experience ranged between the politician and the feminist. It needed to be viewed as a positive gain and not the other way around, especially since us women do not have solid and long-term experience in the field of organization and collective practice.

In the face of how powerful things were as they took the form of the mundane, we continued to live through a period of crisis without the appropriate discourse that could capture what we were going through every day, shed light on the specifics, and point to a personalized awareness and ebullient language. Nothing like that was there, but something of it had started to appear on the horizon. My mother, Rabiha, was the one who abruptly ended this whole crisis. The event is still etched into my memory, but whenever I retell it, it seems fresh and new. My mother, Rabiha's days consisted of nothing more than standing in a line of women cutting pieces of fish for canning. My mother joined the party when Mehmad insisted that she come and bring some other women, but she never told anyone. The covered truck transported their bodies like stacked pieces of wood, and their exhaustion was obvious. But she knocked on the back window to get the driver's attention as she pointed to a spot by the side of the road.

"Leave me next to the party placard, please."

"Are you sure? Everything alright?" The women turned to her peppering her with questions.

"Everything's fine. I'm just going to do what's right. Some professor is coming from the capital and Mehmad told me to come. He made sure three times that I was coming."

The meeting was open to the public, but despite that, the hall was only big enough for party members and some sympathizers. We turned around when we heard the swish of heavy steps mixed with the sardine smell emanating from the timeworn haik and from her entire body. My mother, Rabiha's body still had a swagger that was garbed in confidence and pride, despite the fatigue that hung from her face. Despite her weariness and despite her advanced age, there was still a glow surrounding this woman. She let her eyes wander around the hall and gave a spontaneous greeting. She walked to the second to last row. She dragged a chair toward her after putting her basket to the side and dropped down onto the chair. A body whose very shadow revealed how tired it was. Hours of toil reproducing itself to draw swollen pockets underneath her eyes and cracks all over her hands. But nothing could hold back the glow from her eyes, from her entire face.

I wasn't more than a row from her when she turned to me with a question as soon as the speaker entered.

"That's the professor?"

"Yes, it is."

"He came from the capital?"

"That's right."

"Poor guy. And how long is he going to keep us here?"

"According to the program, three or four hours," I answered, barely able to suppress my laughter.

"Oh my God, what does Mehmad want with me when I have to get up at five in the morning for work?!"

The speaker sat down. To his right sat members of the regional office, one of whom presented him to the audience. He spoke of the importance of the presentation's subject which was established by preparing to engage in community mobility, and how the presentation would monitor the role of the intelligentsia in the process of engagement. He finished by handing the microphone to "the professor," as my mother referred to him. He began with a pure theoretical framing around the intelligentsia in Marxist literature and focused on selections of Gramsci before moving on to the role of the intelligentsia in this country and how it gets along with politicians at this stage. The presentation lasted about an hour and a half. Every once in a while, I turned to steal a glance at my mother who kept sighing, passing her hand over her mouth, her head nodding back a bit. The woman slept fitfully.

She was exhausted. The presentation ended and I thought she would leave as soon as it was over, but she remained glued to her chair. Maybe she knew that leaving before the others would mean Mehmad would lose out on the point he wanted to make by having her come. Maybe.

The floor was opened for questions and comments, of which there were a few. Mehmad's voice came to us alerting us to the fact that there was a finger raised in back. I turned and there was my mother, Rabiha, raising her hand, fingers outstretched. Her questions still ring in my ears.

"Thank you to the professor for what he has said. You talked a lot about the intelligentsia, but you didn't say how this impotence of his would be cured. With a doctor or *fqih* or what? And another question: This Gramsci, from France . . . Does he have any connection to the *fqih*, Germachi, who lives next to us? Or is it just the same name?"

The hall shook and the confusion hung in the air. The intelligentsia, as far as my mother was concerned, was nothing more than a sexual problem (confusing the word *intelligentsia* with *impotence*), and anything foreign was in France. For her, Italy and England were just French cities. If we searched for his family roots, surely, we would find that Gramsci was closely related to the *fqih* Germachi, and if so, my mother would insist that Germachi's prescription was ineffective in solving the problem of impotence, underscoring the fact that impotence was something that happened to men all the time. As for us women, God has spared us of it. She said her piece, then she slipped out of the room.

I only told that story rarely. I carried it with me, rumbling inside for whenever discussion on a specific topic shifted to something theoretically and conceptually vague. The story of my mother, Rabiha, came to me while I was still paddling around in the sea of memories. How could I move on to the best thing in the worst situation? After more than two weeks in the police station, and after growing a bit more accustomed to the different types of torture I faced, I began to resort to muttering at the start of every morning I don't see, a morning of crushing oppression: "Here it is, getting closer." Then I take cover before they arrive with their mask of indifference and deceit by analyzing things with their historical roots and official, Makhzen-esque authenticity. Then I leaned over my body and took a close look. I was beginning to worry quite a bit about it. My breasts had become noticeably swollen and the veins in them had become more prominent. I had never seen them this swollen before. I was afraid they might burst. Whenever they approached, they insisted on trying to convince me to put my signature to the fact that I knew everything about this country. And I would repeat to myself that I truly did know everything, but only about the lines drawn on my body, here on my self. I leaned on my naked wounds. I glimpsed my body's glow, but the glow that hung from a tree of sadness, not an apple tree. It was the same sadness I took from Zahra's eyes when I would visit her, one I could not erase or lessen. When I decided to visit her, it wasn't because of my political orientation; the organization didn't include me, and I didn't have it in me to be disciplined enough for an orientation or a decision on this level. In fact, my relationship with many of the college comrades had started to be seized with reservations. But Zahra was arrested according to a specific orientation, and I would make every effort to visit her on the pretense that her comrades were asking about her, that I was visiting at their request, and because I missed her. I had to clear the air between the two sides. I didn't bring up the other side as much as I cared about Zahra who had begun to be worn down by the rusty mechanisms of her comrades' tongues . . . As soon as she was arrested, she was put into the R4 and driven around Daoudiate, a neighborhood where all the students who the university dorms could not accommodate lived. With Zahra sitting in the car, the agents would park in front of the comrades' housing units and go in looking for them, rifling through their things. Zahra, who spent more than two years in the Chekarem municipal prison, found that she had lost everything right after her release and before the trial. Suspicions about her rained down. The poor woman had drunk from the plague of stabbing, because, according to her comrades, Zahra was the one who had pointed out their houses. The smear campaign against her was systematic and her comrades fell right into the trap. I had to clear the air a bit just for Zahra. What she needed most was my comrades' support, so I built her that imaginary support.

It was cold and damp where, as soon as the blindfold was removed, I found they had thrown me. I smelled moist dirt and knew that I was on the ground, that they hadn't taken me to another detention center or to prison. I couldn't bear the bright light so soon after they had removed the blindfold. Whenever I tried to open my eyes I had to snap them shut again. The beams of light pierced my eyes like needles. I crumpled to the ground where I was after the car had driven off. Only then was I struck by a childlike joy. I remembered my shoes that they hadn't handed me, and I began to rub my eyes to get rid of the fog of the blindfold. In those July days, they threw me out in the same way, except now I would return home on foot, perhaps barefoot. As for that July day that was starting to fade away, I had to dig through my memory for an address to pull myself back together again, to wash off the filth, no questions asked. I wanted to put it all behind me as much as I could. I had no need for a statement or solidarity or scandal. I just wanted to arrange my self that they had scattered all over the sidewalk that dawn.

Lucette was a French nun who came to mind. I didn't know how she ended up in this country. She had worked as a nurse, retired, and stayed here. Lucette made her way into every part of the city. She knew everything about it, including the problems of its women and children. She taught children French with the proper pronunciation. She taught women how to sew.

And on Saturdays and Sundays, she welcomed regiments of monks to perform their group prayers and hold meetings. Her house was elegant. It resembled a church, arranged simply and soothingly. She opened the door for me and as much as she tried to hide her surprise at my early morning visit, she revealed how astonished she was at my condition, the yellow pallor on my face.

She took me by the hand and I went in. She sat me down in a room with a bed and some pillows thrown on a rug on the floor, a table and chair close to the edge of the bed. She asked me what I needed, and I asked if I could use the bathroom. Her mouth wide open, she answered me.

"Why not?"

I didn't know what she meant right then, but after a full day of sleep and waking up to drink a bit of broth, I told her that broth wasn't enough. Hunger was gnawing away at me. She prepared a full meal and sat in front of me. She opened a medicine bottle and said, "These drops will stop the blood flow, and are good for after an abortion." Lucette thought that I had had an abortion and that my pallor and profuse bleeding was a natural result of the fear and nervous tension that put pressure on a woman's psychology, resulting in complications, especially when the pregnancy was outside of marriage. I didn't correct her. I let it slide. Justifying myself was the last thing I would do. What I needed right then was to fill my belly and have a good sleep. I took the medicine bottle. I thanked Lucette. I read the label, smiled, then put it aside. I picked at what was left of the food, then went back to bed, still feeling out of sorts. I stared at the ceiling. I turned off the light as I gathered my wounds, and wondered how many women slept on their sorrows every day.

15

My eyes got somewhat used to the circle of light floating above my head, so I opened them after opening and shutting them for more than an hour. I had been thrown out into an empty, barren space. I saw my shoe there thrown next to me which made me happy. I grabbed it. I tried putting it on but couldn't. My feet were swollen. The shoe seemed too small. I had to push down hard just to get the front half of the foot in. I stood up to the echo of a train whistle and realized where I was. It would take me at least two and a half hours of walking to get to my house. When they arrested me, I had left my purse with a friend who worked in the same office with me at the Arabization Institute. That meant I had neither keys nor money on me. If I found that Mohammed had left for work, how would I get into the apartment? I am the one who, if you had given me a choice at that hour between the present and the future, I would say "good luck to you and your dreams for the future." All *I* needed was a hot shower to wash away the awful smells coming off me, and a toothbrush and toothpaste. As the sour smell enveloped and floated around me, I pressed the doorbell. No sooner had I lifted my finger from the buzzer than I felt footsteps rushing toward me from behind. Mohammed's voice came to me. He couldn't believe it as he threw himself on me and embraced me. I was in desperate need of a hug. I wanted to fall into his arms and cry, but I was exhausted. My breath was labored. He hugged me. He kissed me. I moved my mouth away. I had not brushed my teeth in more than a month. Mohammed carried me into the apartment in his arms after kicking the door open.

Mohammed was close to my pain, to my wounds and to my heart, because he had been there since the beginning, or rather, the end of the beginning. If Mohammed had stayed by my side, with no strings attached, we would still be together. I felt safe with Mohammed, but he couldn't bear my detention. He couldn't stand it that I was sleeping far from him, not for one day, but for forty-five days, and where? With the agents!! Mohammed used to say this secretly, then he began to say it out loud. He was a close support, but he was unable to support me while I was being tossed around in this country's detention centers. On the second day, when he grabbed my body, Mohammed seemed hesitant despite how much we longed for one another. He was scared. Rather, he was disgusted by a body he had revered before, but had then been pissed all over by the agents. I didn't tell Mohammed the details of what the agents had done in his kingdom, so he was left to guess. He might have imagined the worst. I don't know how crazy I was that night, grabbing him all over, embracing him, devouring him like never before. Perhaps whenever we feel hesitant to hold onto one another and we sense the beginning of loss, we throw ourselves more fiercely at what we are losing. I became someone else. Our two bodies became one. Mohammed's body immediately collapsed afterwards, as if he had been pricked in the back with a pin. Oh God! Had I arrived at love too late? And when I knocked, was it as if I had knocked on the wrong door?! How could I bow down and kiss the roots of this sorrow within me? How could I search for rootlessness in my blood? Who would believe me if I were to say that *that* night, I was a heart that spanned nations, wide enough to contain all the hopes of the world's children, yet when the processions of African children arrived, the heart remained silent. Imagine me that night, counting and calculating all of Mutanabbi's words in order to find their essence, and when it finally came to me from among thousands, Mutanabbi comes along to create yet more essences. Imagine me that night, a detainee serving a life sentence whose only dream was to put a sperm into a woman's womb, for the sperm to grow and for a son to come, and when that detainee awakens, he discovers that the mother of his son is a woman he was never married to. Imagine me returning from a school trip and all I want to do is open the door, throw myself inside, and fall into a deep sleep, but when I arrive, I find that I have put the key into the pocket of one of the other children. Who is he? Who is she? I don't know. Imagine me that night and imagine the one shouting at the top of their lungs trying to fend off the crowds as they scream "Your sister's a whore." And that person responds, not to prove that his sister is innocent, but that he doesn't have a sister at all.

I used to know Mohammed well. I knew what he was capable of, which became greater when we joined our bodies together. He would exhaust me. I had discussed that with him before. I insisted that we had to regulate our sex life, and he would always stop me as he laughed, clinging to his rights that were guaranteed by his forefathers and certified by the law.

That night, I felt doubly ashamed. I didn't close my eyes. It was as if I were still in the detention center. I decided to go out to the living room, but then immediately changed my mind. I was scared. Of what? I don't know. But when Mohammed came home from work that evening, he found that I had moved the single bed we had put out on the balcony, which had been Mohammed's bed before we got married. I had brought it into the living room which I had rearranged to make space for it. That's how many of the bonds between Mohammed and I started to come apart. Mutual understanding on more than one level might join two people together, but sex is the umbilical cord that exists between a man and a woman, the thing that ties all the other levels together. Our relationship started to break apart like a piece of pottery whose cracks have started to allow water to seep through. After that, one might repair the clay surface, but there was no hope of getting it to all stick together again no matter how hard one might try.

And so, Mohammed and I split up. Two and a half months after my release, there was no other choice. I was dripping sadness and didn't want to ruminate over its scars more than I already had.

The personal status judge could not accept our decision to separate as we sat there requesting it together. We sat in front of him in silence, stealing glances at one another as if we were on a first date.

The judge tried to recite his Qur'anic verses for us. We listened for a bit. Neither one of us could stop him because so much emotion still required some time to process. Both of us were torn up and in pain. I stole a glance at Mohammed's face. He looked pale. We were no longer listening to the judge as he emphasized the fact that the most hateful halal thing in God's eyes was divorce. I realized that Mohammed was not going to speak. In fact, he might not have heard. Yes, we were both still listening to the heartbeats that extended out between us, but the language of communication had been severed, or, rather, it was broken, until the judge's voice reached us.

"So, what have you decided?"

"We're sticking to our decision."

I answered him as I lowered my eyes to the floor and saw Mohammed raise his broken eyes to me. I said it as I gathered all I had left, and if I hadn't, I would have died. I didn't want to be subject to Mohammed's pleading eyes. All he was asking for was a little more time so we might heal the love between us. The judge didn't pay any attention to my answer and asked the question again, but this time directing his question only at Mohammed.

"Yes," said Mohammed. He pronounced it reluctantly. He asked again and Mohammed again confirmed it mixed with deep sighs. He pulled his body up from the chair, put his hands in his pocket, and remained standing there, as if to hurry the judge to end it. He got ready to leave.

That's how we separated and that's how we left, walking side by side. I felt like crying, sadness preying on a section of my heart. Mohammed might have felt the same way. We continued to drag our feet until we arrived at the Café Mona Lisa. Mohammed invited me in and I accepted. It was silent, perhaps grieving our separation in solidarity with us. I had a black tea. We continued to steal glances at one another even though there weren't many customers in there as it was a workday. We felt suffocated in the café, which was unusual for us.

Mohammed insisted I keep the apartment. He would work something out with one of his friends. He returned just twice to gather up his unfinished paintings and clothes. Then he slipped out of my life. But his things remained. His books and household items, all of them were here, which is what acted as a deposit of sorts here in my heart. My arrest came two months after our divorce. I was presented directly to the court with a file that was empty and heavy at the same time. To this day I don't understand the nature of the charges. All I know is that I was included among a group that was involved in the latest popular uprising, the case having been left open so that "loose threads" could continue to be tied up.

During the two years of my sentence, Mohammed didn't visit me at all. I didn't know anything about what was going on with him. But when my sister, Farida, visited, I insisted she take my housekey that the prison administration had among my private belongings and return it to him and thank him on my behalf.

Mohammed knew about my arrest and how long I had been sentenced for, but he submitted his retirement and emigrated to France. This is all Farida said to me as she opened her purse to put my keys back in.

I didn't know a thing about Mohammed anymore. He was a phantom that was with me from time to time in prison, but one that refused to reappear. That exhausted me to the point that one day I decided to extinguish what remained of my heart, or close it off right here, underneath the arteries, making it feel even more wrung out.

My family divvyed up the visits so that I would receive four visits per month. That is how they would come to the Chekarem municipal prison over the course of two years. My sisters, who understood the particulars of my arrest better than anyone else, were fixtures during all the visits. My father couldn't handle my arrest and one of them always had to be there with him to lighten the mood. That's right, Tali'! I was the youngest of my sisters, the last of the bunch, as they say. My mother kept crying when the sentence was pronounced. My sisters consoled her, but they could not hide their tension and the tears in their eyes. Farida was the one who pointed to me and with her beautiful eyes filled with tears, said, "How can this child have grown up so quickly? How did she go from being such a pampered little girl to finding herself in so much trouble?" All of this created a deep discontent with the injustice that existed in this country.

Everyone surrounded me with double the love. They all asked about me: my uncles, the neighbors, my entire family. I was sitting cross-legged on a throne of tenderness that propped me up. I don't know how it is that I only noticed my relationship with my family after I arrived here. Often, I tried to go out to them in my full elegance but my mother's black djellaba held me back. I knew from before what her favorite colors were. I wanted to joke with her to lighten the mood a little. I grabbed her hands between the bars.

"What's with the black? Where's the henna and kohl on the eyes?"

She smiled, trying to hide her tears.

"Because we're in mourning. How could I wear colors and . . .?"

Her eyes filled with tears. She wiped them and wrung her hands. She put her mouth through the bars and kissed me. Some of the salty tears are still stuck in my throat. But for two years, I couldn't break through my father's sadness. I couldn't meet his eyes for more than a second whenever he visited. I was the one who lowered my eyes from my father's. As for him, he kept looking for things, and more things, in me. Whatever it was he was looking for, I have no idea.

He carried an intense sadness every time he visited me. I asked Farida to convince him to visit every three months so the distance wouldn't tire him out, but what I really wanted was to keep his sadness away from me. It hung there every second he stood in front of me. He didn't talk to me. He just looked at me. Looking was enough, as if it was the second to last time he would ever see me. How could he have closed his eyes one evening to wake up the next morning with me having been arrested? Despite my marriage to Mohammed, despite having graduated from school, I was still the little girl who always needed special care from him and my sisters. When I surrounded myself with obligations, I found myself in a very natural state. I only worked toward self-exploration. But as soon as I came home for summer break, I would fold myself up, or rather, my family would fold me up. I was a white sheet of paper folded in two. During the school year and outside of my home city, I would write with my own hand, but during the summer, they would write me. Prison revealed the beautiful and bright face of my family here in the innermost folds of my heart. Before, I didn't have enough time to look for it or even pay attention to it, even though it was always there. My family was one of three things Safia asked me about as soon as they brought me to Chekarem municipal prison. The guard in her blue uniform grabbed me from the prison administration after I had left some money, my ID card, and my ring with "*la griffe*" ("the claw"), which is what we called the officer who held the keys. The guard brought me to the end of the corridor and the first prisoner whose eye I caught immediately screamed at the top of her lungs,

"Fresh meat!" The women came out from the ward and gathered. I didn't really know what was meant by those two words, but I felt that I was the target. I was still out of sorts despite the long trip between my city and the municipal prison in Chekarem. There was still something of my family's reaction buzzing in my ear from when the agents plucked me from them. My family still didn't know about my divorce from Mohammed. It was no more than a day and a half after I arrived that the guards came to cause the dove even more desperation by choking off its ability to coo. That's why I was distracted. I dragged my steps down the endless corridor when she extended a hand to pull me gently. It was Safia. That was the name of a forty-year old woman who displayed many motherly features. I felt a tacit connection with her from the moment she asked me about the charge, what city I was from, and about my family. Naturally her last question surprised me, as vague as it seemed, but after the bonds had begun to strengthen between us, I knew it was the most important question each new prisoner was asked. It was the entry point to knowing whether I would be productive or merely a dependent of the "tribe," since the women's ward consisted of four tribes. That's what the groups were called. Each tribe included close to a hundred prisoners, and each one was headed by a chief who wasn't elected by the members of the tribe. Rather she imposed herself and wrested the leadership that was usually held by the prisoner with the longest sentence, including life and death sentences. The tribal system here in the ward was not itself free of hierarchy. Some members of these four tribes might try to rebel against, or sometimes even leave the tribal system in order to form smaller groups, but they would not last long. They would soon die out and melt again into one of the tribes that were always at the ready to pounce and devour these smaller ones. All the chiefs of the ward's tribes absolutely denied self-independence for these small rebellious groups.

I had to get used to the general atmosphere of the ward. Insofar as it was imposed that I had no choice, I felt a desire and curiosity to plunge into the worlds of the women's ward. We were living as a society that had inherited much from the hierarchical structures of the outside. Safia convinced me to join her tribe. I found her nature and her ample calm so soothing. Safia was in her forties, medium height, white like a piece of ice wrapped in jet-black hair and eyes filled with the scent of words she only said half of. Despite the nastiness and excessive strictness the job of presiding over the tribe some-times required, Safia was different than the other ward chiefs. She was a sea of tenderness, and I would benefit especially from that. Before even getting up the nerve to ask her why she was arrested, I rejected the possibility that she was in on the same charges the other prisoners were in for. I was betting on some exceptional event having brought this woman here to prison. But I found out that just as she was in charge of a tribe in the ward, Safia headed a gang of gold thieves in Casablanca. The court gave her seven years, and it wasn't her first arrest. In fact, no sooner would the woman get out of prison would she go back in; because theft is a job done every day, and the head of the gang participates in the work in real terms. Her leadership role was defined by a great mastery of the city's geography, and in planning and storage. However, she suffered a lot during her last, bitter stint in prison. Her husband and son had died on their way to visit her. I don't know why the Ministry of Justice didn't offer to reduce her sentence as a way to offer their condolences, which was some-thing that was done a lot. I asked my question again and she told me why she was there.

"Do you steal, Safia?"

"In order to live."

"And are you really the head of a gang?"

"I was the head of two gangs, but one of them fell apart while I was in prison. The other one's still working, and my place is waiting for me. My second-in-command is giving the orders now until I get out."

Just like that and with rare simplicity, Safia explained the nature of her work to me. When she arrived at the Chekarem municipal prison, she had just a year left in her sentence. She was looking forward to finishing that year so she could get some work. Safia had a rare penchant for organizing her group and creating a certain level of intimacy among its members. All of this was a point of pride for Safia with her tribe. But her pride was doubled when she pointed out that hers was the only tribe that included a detainee made from another clay. To be specific, Safia pointed at me and warmly held onto my hand. I said to her,

"Do you know what we'll call this stable tribe, Safia?"

"What?"

"Albania."

"Does Albania look like us?"

"In the stability of the group at any given stage, and in the lack of in-fighting, I say 'yes, it looks like us.'"

The women of Safia's tribe burst out trilling and singing: "Albania, my rose, may the dew fall on you." As soon as their voices started to fade, they rose up again as if they had discovered something new. They pointed to the Khaira group, laughing and saying, "This is the Japan Tribe." They kept repeating the name and punctuating it with laughter as they affirmed that it was a tribe whose need for lentils and tea was ever-growing. I have no idea how the women of the ward had settled upon this image of Japan. Naouma walked into the ward carrying a piece of soap, and as soon as they saw her, they shouted,

"Of course, Naouma, we'll call your tribe the Warrior Tribe."

Naouma was the head of the tribe most beset with problems. Naouma was known as the "box lady." Thirty-five years old (or that's what it seemed), with a long face and wheat-colored skin. Excessively thin. Addicted to coffee and cigarettes. As soon as you looked into her eyes, you sensed something unusual, if not evil, coming from them. They contained sparks you feared might burn you, which made you back away from her. Her tongue was a whip that fell on everyone who passed by her. The language she used was nasty, nauseating. Everyone here avoided running into her. I would cover my eyes with a book when she came into the yard. I had started to prepare for the exam after my request to register for Law School had been approved. I don't know why I felt it necessary to know the law when I was representing myself in front of the judiciary during my trial. As if merely knowing it would push away all this injustice that surrounded me.

16

I WAS FLAT ON MY belly in the prison courtyard, my head in a book, when I felt Naouma's footsteps approaching. I ignored her, although not really. I turned slightly from the book to look at her. I took a notebook from next to me and flipped through the pages to read some of what was written there. I lifted my face to hers. I smiled. She took that as a sign of encouragement and lowered her body to sit down next to me. She began to tell her story without any prompting. I was transfixed. Naouma, who had killed a woman in her ninth month of pregnancy along with her six-year old child, was confessing to her crime. She met her in the hammam, bristling with gold. That's what excited Naouma and prompted her to approach her. She brought her water and rubbed her back and swollen belly which was about to explode. Naouma was still in her fourth month. "I had to invite her to drink a cup of coffee with me as we walked home from the hammam. I insisted and she agreed. That's how I killed the mother and the fetus in her belly, along with her little girl. I slaughtered them, cut them into pieces, and fried them so their flesh wouldn't rot too quickly.

"I did it all with the help of my husband, Ayyache. We put them in a medium-sized box, tied it up well, and sent it out to where the ocean is. We don't have an ocean here. But for the first time, the agent was unable to receive the goods, so they didn't get to the ocean. They were returned to Chekarem where they started to stink up the garage and . . . anyway . . . Of course, my husband, Ayyache, he's the one who pushed me into committing this last crime. I'm the one who caught the victim, but he helped me execute every step of the plan. When they arrested us, he convinced me to declare his innocence. He explained that the police would let me go because I was pregnant, and that even if I did go to prison, it wouldn't be for long for the same reason. I declared Ayyache's innocence, and, over the course of the investigation, I felt compelled to drag in anyone with whom I had had the slightest misunderstanding; my neighbors who I argued with, the neighborhood grocer, the hammam worker, the carpenter who strung me along on account of a small table for three months . . ." Naouma went down the list with a diabolical laugh. Then she stopped. Her eyes darted around a little as she rubbed one hand with the other, adding,

"Mohammed, the boy, is innocent, there's no denying it. I used to love him like crazy. We had a sexual relationship for some time before I met Ayyache. I asked him to marry me, but he refused. When I got married, I continued to pursue him. I still loved him even though he kept rejecting me. When I was sent to prison, I thought about him a lot. My heart continued to swing between something I still had for him here inside me and his constant rejection of me. I settled on the latter. Out of revenge, I implicated him in the murder which was easy since he lived close to the victim. I told them he was the one who had led me to her. Of course, I held fast to that line for the duration of the three-year investigation, saying that he was my number one partner in the operation. Now he's there in the Gharbia municipal prison, sentenced to die like me. Just like me."

When she pronounced the words "sentenced to die" in reference to the boy, Naouma roared with laughter, which is what she did when she was placed among the prisoners too. They would argue, pull hair, and scream while she stood in a nearby corner watching and laughing. That's Naouma. A sadistic woman par excellence. In fact, when she was to blame for one of the prisoners cracking, you would see her slink over to make sure with her own eyes that the matter was over and done with. Her group experienced constant disturbances and never-ending problems. As soon as Safia was released from prison, I was immediately granted leadership of her tribe at the urging of all of Albania's women, even though my sentence was shorter than theirs. Naouma tried as hard as she could to incorporate my group into her kingdom. She dreamed of notoriety and did not hide her aspirations that she would one day become the head of an empire into which the four groups would dissolve. She used to laugh and say, "One day you'll go to sleep and wake up to Naouma. That's right! Naouma. Everything from now on will pass, but Naouma's beautifully radiant face will remain. That's right . . . one morning I'll snatch up leadership of all the tribes. You'll see."

Precious few were the moments of pure cheerfulness that Naouma might live. Few were the moments of reconciliation with the self, of leaning on it, even listening to it. One such moment was when she was finished or was preparing to meet her boyfriend, Sibai, who she fell in love with here, inside the prison. Naouma said that he loved her too. He was serving a life sentence. Naouma refused to wear the prison uniform just as she refused to put a veil on over her hair. She always looked elegant. There was someone who supported the relationship between Naouma and her lover, Sibai, and who made arrangements for her to get together with him. How? I don't know. But Naouma, who supposedly stayed up late washing the clothes of all the guards' families here in the prison would get the credit for it and this doubled as a ladder with which she reached her boyfriend. In fact, the prisoners of her tribe were the ones who did the washing, despite themselves. Perhaps Sibai performed other types of services for the male guards. Naouma returned from her romantic trysts humming and singing snippets of Oum Kulthoum. This was one of those moments that escaped the grip of her machinations, when we felt that there was another side to this woman. That is, before a fight flared up with Yamna, chief of the rug-producing tribe, for no other reason than the fact that Naouma didn't like Yamna who was brown-skinned, short, with frizzy hair and squinty eyes. That was how she explained her quarrels with Yamna, even though the reason was bigger than that. Yamna was a master rug maker according to the guards and all the women of the ward. This had been the guard's task, but she gave it to Yamna then would head off to the office for some chitchat. Yamna was an expert in weaving all types of rugs, which qualified her to become head of the entire ward, and that's what made Naouma so angry. Poor Yamna, sentenced to twenty years, was always requesting that she be transferred to another prison of her choosing. But as soon as the guard in charge of rug-making would learn about her having written up the request (and she would learn about it through a whisper from Naouma) she would tear it up before it ever reached the warden's office. The guard knew that if Yamna left, the burden of teaching the prisoners how to weave would fall to *her* every day. But Yamna was smart, and she asked one of her visiting relatives to send the transfer request from outside the prison. It was accepted a month later. The guard practically fainted when she received the news. She went up to Yamna threatening, "Don't be too happy. I'll get you back here, by force if I have to."

Yamna left, and in her pure heart she held a bit of fear of the guard's threats. By this time, she had served half her sentence. Yamna was hoping to spend what remained of her time moving from one prison to another. She often explained this desire of hers saying,

"I'll just go from prison to prison and the ten years will pass without having felt them at all."

We laughed when we heard Yamna's explanation just as we laughed when she made plans to limit her group to Berber prisoners. What more did one need to accuse her of racism and factionalism?! But Yamna would laugh long and hard and say to me, "Even though I don't understand what these words mean, I know they aren't exactly complimentary." Yamna defended her position by explaining that she wasn't very good at Arabic, nor was she prepared to learn it. "I don't have time to learn Arabic." Even after Yamna left, we still heard Amazigh songs inside the rug workshop, along with thunderously loud trills.

No one in prison can understand that a political detainee has anything to do with them, these exhausted masses. They always look suspiciously at political detainees as if they have some sort of a connection to power. I, for example, am here because I am against authority and want to replace it with *my* authority. But in the eyes of the regular prisoners, this does not at all mean that these political detainees who are scattered throughout the country's prisons are there paying the price out of love for those prisoners. To the regular prisoner, the political detainee's love is only for herself. And only *we* are able to swallow this talk and easily chew it without realizing that those we are talking about are not represented by it. In fact, they can't stand it. The distance is vast. A chasm that cannot be filled with just words. That's how the relationship between the Left and the opposition to these masses seemed to me. I didn't imagine that I would enter into a constant state of alert to defend my identity here in prison. When I was being held in secret detention, even during the trial, I felt that what I was doing was insignificant when compared to how much torture they were inflicting on me, and how serious the accusations were. So, at first, I said to myself how happy I was that "I was involved in something big." That's what I said to myself when I saw the charges wrapping themselves around me. But as soon as I arrived at the Chekarem municipal prison after the sentence was handed down, I was transformed into a series of sparks that spewed in every direction when I tried to pull back any piece there was of my identity. I underlined it in red. Daily life in the women's ward experienced constant troubles and upheavals that pushed relationships to their worst. The reading lessons I had started with Safia and ten other women who had never deciphered a letter became, according to the smears of the prison warden, a political cell that I was using to incite unrest. I lost my cool and defended it with everything I had, but soon realized I didn't have anything at all. That's how prison is. As soon as you're thrown in, you feel a sharp pair of scissors cutting out a large part of your dignity. In fact, I felt that the prison machine was intent on humiliating us for the rest of our lives. Once I asked myself: Are these the masses for whom we pay so dearly with our lives? Much of the fresh purity I had used to sketch them here inside me had started to dry up and turn brittle. I didn't emerge from my silent grief until that night, dragged out of it by all the gossiping on the ward. Groups of women approached me asking for details about what I saw that night. They crowded around on Omar Street (which is what they called the long corridor that separated the ward from the prison yard) winking and whispering to one another.

I did not have the slightest desire to describe what I saw, but it was clear that the other prisoners in the women's ward had already seen it. However, because they tried to avoid Fat Zubaida's evil, they could not show the slightest reaction. I am not at all sure of the two women's faces. I looked closely at them but could not grasp their features. When I woke up in the middle of the night to the moaning of one of the women whose bed was close to mine, at first, I thought it was Fatna Jilali whose moaning preceded the onset of a pain that would culminate in severe nervous fits. The woman habitually writhed around in every bed in the ward despite the prisoners' protests. To avoid conflicts with her, the women would give in and leave their beds one after the other every night according to Fatna Jilali's wishes. I opened my eyes then closed them again, but I could still hear the moaning, coming from somewhere deep in the night. I opened my eyes again and fixed them on the spot where the moaning was coming from. It was not a moan of pain, and Fatna Jilali was not sleeping here in the bed close to mine. It was a moan of pleasure and lust, and the body was actually two naked bodies intertwined—a fat body, massive, on top and one that looked thin underneath it. A hand with swollen fingers slipped over the thin body that raised its head up and sighed. My eyes were transfixed on the fat hand with the swollen fingers. It looked like a broom stretched out to sweep something up before moving down to the thighs in search of something. The thin body still shook under the touches of the fat hand, its head buried in the thick hair of the fat woman. I looked closely. I lifted my head up a little bit from my pillow. I heard her whisper soft words that made the slender body shake with desire and the two of them started to rub against one another more quickly. I was still rubbing my eyes, bleary from the surprise when I stood on my bed and yelled as loudly as I could,

"Oh, come on! For crying out loud!"

Then a voice pushed back from the depths of the ward, holding me back as if to protect me.

"Go to sleep, you ugly cow!"

The voice did not try to shut me up just once. Rather it repeated itself more than three times. I felt an electricity in the room. I turned toward the wall and tried to go back to sleep, but I couldn't. Every time I closed my eyes, the image was right there in front of me. I turned again and saw that the two bodies had pulled apart, fatigue and exertion showing in their repose. Safia told me that the huge body was Fat Zubaida. But what they didn't catch was the woman who was having sex with Zubaida. They suspected it was Naouma, the "box-lady." That's why the woman at the other side of the ward was trying to keep me from yelling out, in order to stand between me and the evil of these two women. I did not believe it was Naouma because the thin woman underneath Fat Zubaida was short. Ever since Naouma had told me the details of her crime and how she confessed to it, I didn't know what to make of her love and sex life, even when she talked about Sibai. I considered it unlikely that there had been a man in this woman's life. The poor woman commuted the death sentence that hadn't yet been transformed into a life sentence through sheer imagination and illusion. Naouma kills. A woman has sex with another. And gives birth to a girl.

When I asked Safia about Fat Zubaida, she laughed and said, "That woman hasn't been near a man in forever."

I insisted on knowing the reason and learned that Zubaida had been married less than two years when her husband went to work in Italy, leaving her behind in the house of her father-in-law. The old man would wait for night to fall over the large family house and for silence to settle in, then he would get up and slink into Zubaida's, his son's wife's room. Zubaida knew well that he was her husband's father and could imagine how big the scandal would be if she stood up to him and screamed. For more than two weeks, she held him off and defied him until she came to a decision. One evening, she took a scythe from the mint field and placed it under her head. When her father-in-law noticed that Zubaida was not putting up any resistance, he took off his baggy trousers only for Zubaida to surprise him with the scythe and cut off his penis.

It was considered a case of premediated murder. Zubaida got a life sentence and instant divorce papers from her husband.

Whenever Fat Zubaida told the story of what she did to her father-in-law, she did so with bravado and pride, all the while clinging to her innocence, discrediting the judiciary, and calling out the injustice in this country at every opportunity. Zubaiba was someone who embodied two opposites. She slept with a woman at night, and during the day, she insulted, spat on, and pulled the hair of another. But while the nighttime women may have been numerous, there was only one daytime

woman onto whom Fat Zubaida would pour her anger—
Malika, also known as Flip-flop, because we would hear the
echo of her plastic sandals whenever she walked through the
ward. Down the entire length of the corridor, the women of
the ward would yell as she walked by,
        "Pick up your feet. What's all this flip flopping?!"
    All the prisoners who entered the women's prison knew
Malika by her nickname before they knew her actual name.
In fact, there were prisoners who served short sentences and
never even got the chance to know her by her given name.
She was just Flip-flop. I often thought about her hostile relationship with Fat Zubaida, but it stemmed from nothing more
than disgust at what she had done to land her in prison. Even
though prisoners are all framed as such within the general
confines of the law, the charges attached to them are ranked
and hierarchical.
    Before Flip-flop got here, news of her arrival which was
wrapped up in her case had been leaked by the guards to
all the women here in the ward and throughout the prison.
Everyone said the *basmala*, sought strength from God, cursed
Satan, and spat right and left. Malika arrived with her belly
swollen, but that wasn't the problem. Malika was pregnant by
her brother. But although there were whispers about her in
the women's ward from time to time, Flip-flop was eventually
able to integrate, despite the fact that Fat Zubaiba continued
to harrass her. Sometimes we would wake up in the middle of
the night, or even at dawn, to Malika screaming for help freeing her neck from Zubaida's fingernail grip. Thus, Flip-flop
remained a jarring presence, but not as much as her brother
who was both her "husband" and the baby's uncle. The prison
wards stood together with hands intertwined forming a barrier in front of the entrances. Their refusal to let him enter was
absolute, and the administration had to put him in an individual cell. No more than six months passed before he contracted
tuberculosis and died. And it was right around then that the

baby girl was removed from Malika. She didn't know where the French nuns took her but knew well she would never see her again. That's how every once in a while, Zubaida would stir things up with Malika, which led to fights between the heads of two tribes, between Naouma and Khaira. Khaira couldn't stand up too much to Naouma, because as soon as Naouma would start fighting, a thread would threaten to strangle all the women of Khaira's tribe. Whenever the battle started to heat up, Hafida the Hippie would raise her voice to urge the women of the ward to cheer and sing from their beds before then stepping down onto the floor.

> Tomorrow he will be born who puts on full armor,
> who lights the fire completely,
> who seeks vengeance,
> who will bring forth the truth from the ribs of the impossible.

I hardly caught the first snippet before I burst out laughing and the fog of war began to thicken with the troupe starting to dance to Hafida the Hippie's cheering. The prisoners here in the women's ward only knew how to sing. One day, they insisted that *I* sing. I told them I could only recite a bit of poetry. They wondered what poetry meant, then said, "We'll sing it. Just start."

"But without a tune."

"We'll give it a tune, so don't worry about it!"

I recited a passage from "Do not reconcile" by Amal Dunqul for them. They repeated it more than six times in unison. After that, they picked up buckets and plates and began to sing. They didn't settle on a specific tune. They didn't look to one another for guidance. But despite all that, their tune came as one. They began to perform the passage as if they were done rehearsing it and putting it to music, while I was the only one left stammering, as usual. They added and removed what they needed to in order to make the passage fit with the rhythmic bucket-drumming and dancing with scarves tied around their waists to what was left of the passage.

Tomorrow he'll be born who puts on full armor
who'll fully light the fire
who'll seek revenge . . . enge . . . enge
from the ribs of the impossible.

I accepted all the omissions imposed by our dialect, but as soon as they approached the end, the drumming got louder as they yelled "wah wah wah" and I burst out laughing. I rolled around with tears of laughter in my eyes as I saw how the passage had landed, with Naouma gently shaking her body and Safia looking quite attractive with her thick hair, having tucked the long tails of her shirt into her belt, while the rest of the women clapped and drummed on the buckets yelling "wah wah wah." Thus, the women of the ward worked together to slip this passage deep into themselves and raise it up whenever things got difficult, such as when an argument or a quarrel or a sadness overwhelmed us. More than once they surprised me with the passage. Whenever they noticed me withdrawing or secluding myself in one of the courtyard's corners or somewhere in the ward, they would pounce on me with their Dunqul-esque trilling, temporarily pulling me out of my seclusion, in spite of myself. Despite the many reasons each prisoner had for being here, despite the many blows that were struck at all of our relationships, some sort of warmth continued to float up above all the women's heads and deep within us. We had been drawn toward one another. Just as some moments were dark and bleak, shaking us to our very core, there were moments that extended themselves to stitch a glow inside us, so you could imagine that as soon as you put your hand on that glow, all good things followed.

I had no desire to put an end to these relationships that had been born between us. I let them flow freely. Sometimes I tried to put them on ice and take a break just so I could read a little, but when I did, I felt shut off, devastated. I thirsted for the chants and stories of the women in the ward. They had begun receiving letters from their families after we took the initiative to write to them. I came to be asked to write at least two letters a day. We called our families the Organization of Nations. Whenever our internal marketplace ran out, we sought aid by writing up a list of needed supplies and sending it to the Organization of Nations. But the meal that saved us from the error of mass poverty here in the prison was well-known and circulated among the four tribes. All that remained from the week's bread was put into a large plastic bag. We continued to collect it until crisis would start to knock at the ward's door. We would take out our stores of lentils and fava beans and wash the bread and dry it in the sun while we prepared the broth with the lentils and fava beans before then soaking the bread after having torn it up into little pieces. *Terda* was the key to solving the hunger crisis, but it did not mean a thing unless it came with a pot of tea. I will continue to smell that dish forever. Safia was a master at preparing it and I learned from her. I started to gain weight day after day, especially in my rear end. This made the other prisoners mock me, commenting that the goodness lay in the *terda*, but what do you know about *terda*, anyway?

The whole time I was there, Hafida was imprisoned thirteen times. Her sentences were never more than two months if she wasn't released on bail as soon as the sentence was issued. Hafida was a master storyteller, delighting us especially at night. She worked as a tour guide for foreigners, unlicensed though—this country had become so modernized which meant that guiding someone to a street or a specific place had become a profession that required a special permit. Thus, whenever Hafida was rounded up with the other hippies, she was arrested, and no sooner did she walk through the prison gate than did she get her old job back and come right back to us. The prisoners asked her to bring us kohl, siwak, and washcloth mitts when she returned. I used to laugh at these requests that counted on Hafida's imminent return. When Hafida was with us, we could only fall asleep after tucking ourselves in and listening to the story of Aicha Laâbou. Hafida was an amazing storyteller, but when she sensed that we were nodding off and giving in to sleep, she would bellow in a voice that thundered throughout the ward,

"And Aicha Laâbou died!"

We would wake up from the beginnings of a broken sleep to her yelling as she laughed and said,

"And me? Who puts me to sleep, bitches?!"

Hafida didn't call any prisoner by name. In this way, we were all the same to her. No consideration of age, or the dignity of grey hair, or anything else. One day she came up to me as Bint Maâti protested my refusal to go to the administration and make an appointment for her with the prison doctor. Normally I was the ticket that made it possible for the women of the ward to see the doctor and get medication. I often joked with Bint Maâti when she insisted that she needed to see the doctor so he could remove one of her kidneys that was causing her pain. I would get her all riled up by telling her that she needed to seize her right to medical treatment with her own hand. Bint Maâti thought that what I meant was a hunger strike and she got really angry, knowing that it was a form of self-starvation.

"God forbid, we don't even have enough food to start a hunger strike. God forbid, God forbid!"

She poured down insults and cursed a fate that had placed her health into such irresponsible hands. I don't know if she meant me or the others. Only then did I slip out to sign up and no sooner did I leave the clinic nurse than I bumped into Bint Maâti going in, and she ignored me. I burst out laughing and hugged her as I told her that the doctor would be coming the following day. While I was insisting that the doctor come quickly on their behalf, it never occurred to me, during my second month there, that I would become a regular customer at the clinic when pain froze my joints and extended into my lower back. Tests revealed a failure of my right kidney.

When the warden called me in to tell me that the administration would not be able to provide medication for me because of its exorbitant price, and because the administration was still in deep debt to one of the local pharmacies, I didn't ask about the fate of the budget and the many secret paths that led to it. I wasn't going to scream in his face because I knew that the decision to plunge into battle was an uneven bet. However, what I did do was bow my head and say to him, "Ok, I agree to buying the medication . . ." but before a look of relief had had a chance to spread over his face, I continued, ". . .but only if I had the illness before coming to prison. Meaning, I'm not responsible for covering the costs of treating any ailment I might have contracted here." My throat hurt as I spoke. Because we both knew well that the source of my problems was the cold temperature in the prison, not to mention the month I had spent in secret detention. I was hunched over. The warden looked at me for a moment, smiled nicely, and I left. He knew full well that the illness was as new to me as the women's ward, the profanities, Hafida the Hippie's stories, and the scuffling flip-flopping of Malika's plastic sandals.

17

I HEARD THAT THERE WERE seven detainees, members of the Cooperative of the Faculty of Sciences Office, here at the municipal prison. That was further confirmed when their anthems began to fill the air, coming to us in our various spots around the yard. I asked Safia to find out about those student detainees for me; she was close to some of the guards whom she would go and see in their offices in the administration building. Safia was running a bit late when she came to see me. Under her arm she had two newspapers that she threw at me and said over her shoulder as she walked away, "Everything on your friends is here." She pointed to the two newspapers. I took them as if grabbing onto impossible-to-get contraband.

Here on the third page, above the fold, I found some announcements. One of them seemed to have come from here. It carried the signatures of the seven detainees and the name of the prison. I read their names. I didn't know any of them, but their voices resonating through the prison's darkness had become close to me here, to my heart. I read the two newspapers as if grasping onto details of a life that was all but gone. Here, in all these wide pages, I felt a semblance of life. Everything on the outside was still the same size. The same print that left black ink on my hand. A memorial for a martyr here on the bottom half of the page surrounded by real estate listings and advertisements. Fading headlines. One of the prisoners came by urging me to play cards. Normally I would have, but today I declined. I buried my head in the newspapers after pulling the cover over my body. Safia came back to hurry me along so she could return them to the guard who had given them to her from the warden's office. I gave them back and she left, my eyes following her. If not for the poverty and drudgery that had led her to steal gold, what would Safia have become, had she been provided with the conditions of a good life? She was the only one who refused to leave the ward and join the others in the yard on national holidays when they brought everyone out to where the television was placed so we could listen to the official speeches. The king's birthday, the Feast of the Throne, and other special days that required speeches, those were our chances to watch television. We didn't have a radio. The medium- and long-term prisoners considered these two years to be the best years in that we were obliged—as Fat Zubaida put it—to watch television nine times. She kept count of them on her fingers, naming movie titles. How's that? I didn't understand at first. Well, all the women were willing to listen to the television speeches provided they could listen to them again after the final news report. The speech would pass during the main news and the women would raise up their hands, praying that the film that followed the news would be Egyptian. My family never brought me news from the outside except for what had to do with the well-being of family members and neighbors. As for what was going on in the alleyways, streets, avenues, cities, and the rest of the country, I felt a palpable lack in that regard. All I could do was pore over those speeches. I studied them thoroughly. I memorized parts of them. I turned them upside down and from them I fashioned a key to what was going on outside.

For 730 days, no one visited me except for my family and some girlfriends from among the neighbors' daughters. Mohammed's image started to fade from my mind. My heart felt as indifferent as could be. How can I talk about all these internal ruptures? Who would believe me if I pointed to my heart and said that this was a sweet Jaffa orange and deep discontent here in a piece of my heart. I furrowed my brow to grab onto the history of that night, and the date of the martyr, Omar Benjelloun's assassination came to me. Here in this ward that was full of worries, I began to feel it from all sides, urging me to tell you about what the country and its people have become. After whispering to you that I was prepared to write the saddest things that evening, I got lost between the divisions of this country and the details of the story. But who am I to scrape at the scales of fish, or to understand what horses mean when they neigh, or to force the media to commemorate the people from here, from the ward? Who am I to change a river's course, exchange today with tomorrow, and the song of the forest with that of the nation? No, it's just up to me to jot down the highlights for myself. It's up to *you* to take the case of Omar Benjelloun and analyze it in order to deconstruct in it what will absolve me. I won't tell you about a daily newspaper that confounds our research on the martyrs' death toll by burying it among real estate advertisements. Here nothing wants to extend the deadline for us. Neither accumulation, nor struggle, nor complete rupture gathers up its suitcases and leaves unless absolutely final, so they crouch underneath sturdily-built chairs. In fact, even transformation, when we experience it, advances toward us with sharp features that resemble those of defeat. We knew it as we switched from a wide audience to seats in one café after another. I will tell you how we are scattered selves. The more we extend ourselves as a bridge, the more the tools fall, and the mechanism breaks down. So, I slide my body to stand up before resuming, and a question settles on my chest that almost suffocates me: How does the one who belongs to the future become an orphan of belonging to a moment? I loved and savored the future down to its dregs, and now I am drunk with forgetting and with the ability to express something I only possess half of.

I continued to stare at the ceiling. This whole time, I had gotten used to focusing on nothing. I stared at the ceiling, but after having had enough of wandering around lost, tonight, the martyr's memory floats around me. It rises up to the corners of the cell. It sprays me with mist and when the memory starts to fill everything up, I quickly close my eyes, so I am not dragged into a state of intense focus that causes so much pain. I indulge in the hope that when my glass is empty, I will slurp up all of time, yet how is it that my glass is still full? I felt some sweat drip from my forehead, from my whole body, like the day I went into Mouline's bathroom to wash my face that was damp with sweat, but not my sweat. I had slipped out from underneath his body, his teeth chattering, and slinked off to the bathroom. Seeing a number of toothbrushes there, I realized that a kingdom of women had passed through here before me. They left perfume, a toothbrush, sunglasses, cigarette butts, an unmade bed. That's how Mouline was. He would get up, go to the bathroom, and wash himself of the memory of that day's woman so he could welcome the next day's. And before leaving for work, while she stayed behind in the apartment, he would leave her the key and tell her where to put it. But when I took the key, I was left breathless. So, it is in *you* that I will read about all types of women. Your apartment key was a clean sheet of paper from which the traces of a woman, and another, and another emanated. Despite their dainty fingertips, the key was rubbed of its sheen and seemed to have been carved, the color worn off, almost rusted. I passed my hand over the excessive roughness, not wanting to rub clean the kingdom of your women. I didn't want to leave a signature for you in the key either. I locked the door and went down the stairs. I paused. The building's cleaning woman was still lurking, following me with her eyes so she could know which apartment had just spat me out. I threw the key into your wooden mailbox, just as you told me to, with the woman still staring at my back like an amateur detective.

Right then, I wondered how many women had stopped to toss the key in while bristling under the gaze of strangers. How many women had said to themselves, the key slipping from their fingers and falling to the bottom of the wooden box, "If only I could stay upstairs just a while longer"? I know, Mouline, that you are scattered between the scent of different women's perfumes, and I am the one who gathers you up, not with perfume, not by excelling in the arts of passion, not by putting my body on display. This Mouline carries many of Nabil Qozah's traits, especially his silence and his patience. I don't know whether I was searching Mouline for things that reminded me of Nabil, or the opposite, but they're both like fire when it burns your hand, and instead of dreaming of grabbing onto its spark, you rush to throw it to the ground or run away from it. That's how the Lebanese War lost Nabil Qozah. I don't hear from him anymore. He doesn't call me, and I don't hear anything about him. To this day, I don't know how he was swept away: death by bombs or emigration upon emigration? All I had left of Nabil Qozah was a map, drawn by his hand, that clearly laid out Lebanon's body, what ambitions for conquest existed there, and how hostilities between brothers had taken root as a result of the war. This Nabil did not skimp, even with the little details of Lebanon and its borders. While I listened to him, I would steal a glance of his face from time to time. His thick eyebrows that looked like a pine forest, his clear forehead, his broad shoulders. I always imagined Nabil, hunched over as he walked, on an urgent mission. I insisted on moving the blanket from the ground floor of our family home to the second floor.

"Why?"

"Tomorrow's Sunday and the kids will wake up early and fill the alleyways with screaming."

"And what's wrong with that?"

"After staying up so late, it would be best to sleep in a little. The kids' screaming will annoy you."

"Anyone who's used to staying up all night during the war on Mount Lebanon, who's been woken up by the fevered explosions of bombs and gunpowder, unable to close his eyes for two, three, four weeks at a time, will think he's in heaven here with the sounds of kids and birds."

The last time Nabil Qozah visited we were unable to meet. He came from Lebanon by way of Paris after recuperating from various fractures he had suffered in his right hand and back. He was here for just two days. We set a time to meet at the Café Mona Lisa on Hourriya Avenue, but I was surprised that the street had been split in two. I was unaware that the Turkish president, Kenan Evren, was visiting our country. In fact, if not for the labyrinth we had been placed into, I wouldn't even have known the name of Turkey's president! The street was split in two and all the main corridors were fenced off. Nabil was on the east side while I was here on the west side where the Café Mona Lisa was. How would we get through the fencing so we could meet? The blockade lasted for more than four hours, because that's the only way to gather crowds of people and fabricate an official reception for guests.

I went back to the café so that I might console myself by looking for something of Nabil in the face of Malik, the café's Lebanese owner. I didn't see Nabil and it was only later that I heard his voice coming to me from Charles De Gaulle Airport as he prepared to board his flight back to Lebanon. His voice spewed sparks in my ear as I wiped my reticent tears and held onto the receiver cradled between my ear and my shoulder. Nabil kept cursing, enraged that East and West Beiruts were being re-created all over the Arab world.

"What can I say, Leila? I didn't know it would be like Beirut there with you. What were you doing in West Beirut and me in East Beirut, on one street? And on Hourriya Avenue, named for freedom and liberty, no less! Capitals are shuffled like cards. Cards . . ."

I haven't heard Nabil's voice since that day. I haven't heard anything more about him. But something told me that Nabil was lost to the war in Lebanon when it was just getting going. I tried calling some of the numbers I had for him in Paris and Amman, but no one had any news about Nabil. I knew that their magazine had stopped publication. I hadn't seen it here for six months. Nabil told me about how the magazine first got started. When I got it here, it seemed like it had always been large, but we burst into laughter when he pulled out his wallet and showed me a picture of the magazine's headquarters. It was nothing more than a small room inside a ruined house, destroyed at the start of the war. Nabil and his four colleagues whose names he told me, they all looked like relief statues inside a narrow chamber. Surrounded by papers, only their heads were visible. Nabil is still here with me, fresh as the heart of a head of lettuce. Fierce, like a pack of firecrackers that might go off in your hands without any warning. Nabil Qozah put me at ease, but I couldn't slip into every chamber of his spirit. There was no time for that. All Nabil had time for was talking about Lebanon. I saw him, and Lebanon, right here in front of me, exhausted.

In his last, very sad letter to me, he told me of his dream to return one day to his grandfather's house in southern Lebanon, without any barricades or bombs. And when his wounds flowed too thick on paper, he suddenly realized it and sarcastically changed the subject. Ever since I had decided to prepare my thesis and plunge into academic research, Nabil mocked me relentlessly.

"Leila, you're not made for this type of work. What is academic research anyway? The country has advanced, for crying out loud. You, Leila, are running from something specific toward academic research and into a maze. Now you're like the fish that throws itself from the ocean's water to the sweet water of the river, but the fish that's you is really looking for salt to coat its skin, not the sweetness of river water."

Of course, when I decided to stop my dissertation research, it wasn't because I was convinced by what Nabil said. But when I decided to investigate Moukhtar's situation rather than count words, Nabil appeared before me, and I saw that fish again, swimming where the river and ocean meet. I saw it escape and plunge deep into the water of life, here with salt, here in the ocean.

Nabil came from tomorrow's gambles, as far as I was concerned. I never felt that he was from today. No. He was from tomorrow. But time has a way of suddenly revealing that this tomorrow is the biggest cheat of all when it forces us to expect it in a specific form. We draw it a certain way, and no sooner does it grow than it surprises us. It attacks us differently. Completely differently than the way we drew it that day.

18

I ONLY HAD THREE MONTHS to go in my two years here when a veil of sadness descended on me. It enveloped me all the time. It felt like a heavy sadness settling all through me. My family sensed my dejection when they visited me. The more they looked forward to the end of the sentence, the more aloof, even cold I appeared to them, as if I were still in the first days of my detention. I felt an emptiness that my family, the women of the ward, even Nabil and Mohammed (if they were to come) would find impossible to fill. There were voids the effects of which I felt expanding inside me. How could I fill them, having been crushed for two years with no reason for my being here? Despite what my relationship with the comrades of the party had devolved into, despite what had been hollowed out as a chasm between us, I had bet on a support of that sort. Would it be possible for me to one day forgive and condone those who had stabbed me in the back with the dagger of suspicion? Despite the heavy dejection I dragged around, I was motioning to myself, and with myself, that there was still something in my heart that deserved attention. There was no one who could understand the whirlpool I was swirling around in, because that's just the way I was, undisciplined, they said. Two years ago, the organization made me severely dizzy, but I didn't live it the way I had when they spun suspicious accusations around me. As I approached the end of my sentence, I urged myself to assess this experience from here.

But I wasn't at all expecting that someone who had been a comrade would be so bold as to come to me, in my home, with a twelve-page notebook under his arm. As soon as he greeted me, he sat down in front of me. He handed me the notebook and asked, rather, he ordered me rudely, to write my assessment of the detention experience. I was unable to hold myself together, and I asked him,

"Within what framework? In what way? I don't know you."

Reda Lalami was confused. He straightened his glasses. He pulled the notebook toward him across the table and stood up. I noticed that he was shaking and turning in on himself like a hedgehog going into its spiky shell. I tried to lighten the mood a little by saying,

"Concerning me, I did an assessment there while I was in prison, and for now, I consider it mine and mine only. I don't know what in it could possibly interest you all."

He left after bidding me a truncated farewell. I went into my room. I locked the door from the inside and cried with burning pain for everything that had been broken between us. The gall! They only got in touch with me in order to obtain a specific report, and I didn't know what they wanted with it. I didn't even know whether they had asked about me from a distance through my family while I was in prison. I couldn't broach the subject with my brother or sisters because I didn't want to make them feel awkward that they hadn't asked about me. They didn't ask about me while I was in prison, and they come to me now for an assessment of my experience?! What do they care about the experience or about me? I felt so strongly then that time could re-form our beings anew, when it might be a revolutionary formulation of what we had been before. I've never been anything but calm. Never one to get excited or upset. But after my release, I discovered that I had begun to lose many of what everyone considered to be my positive traits, including my calm. I might have become highly volatile. Why? How? I don't know and I'm not required to. It is what it is.

There was nothing new after two years, or at least that's how it seemed to me. I couldn't find anyone to take me by the hand, to fill in the blanks and all the gaps of those two years.

After spending more than a month with my family, I packed my suitcase and got ready to say goodbye to them. I was going to travel to my home, not even knowing if it was still there. I repeated the apartment and building number to myself and smiled. How had I not realized that the sum of the digits in my arrest number gave the exact number of my apartment? I smiled to myself as I took the train ticket and said goodbye to Farida and my mother who insisted on accompanying me to the station. I felt like a child learning how to cross the street for the first time, their mother making sure they look right and left and watching carefully until the hard metal of the cars disappears and they arrive safely across the street. My mother squeezed my hand as she embraced me, holding her tears back until after I had gone. Farida looked like a flower opening in the morning dew. Her face was radiant. I looked closely at her and realized for the first time how beautiful she was. When she speaks to you, Farida uses everything to communicate. Her eyes. Her eyebrows. The movement of her head. Her hands. Even if the subject is cold and mundane, Farida will give it to you with warm and glowing gestures. She asked me to call them to let them know that I arrived, to tell them about the apartment, and whether I had any updates concerning work. I didn't know whether they would keep me in the civil service at the Arabization Institute or whether the criminal record and the talk that would come as a result would prevent it.

When the train let me out, I hesitated for a moment. I saw the #43 bus. I didn't remember where it came from or where it went. I asked one of the people standing at the stop. He told me what direction it was headed, and I realized it was

going to where I lived, or rather, where I used to live. I didn't
know whether I would find the apartment or not. All I had
was the key. I didn't want to exhaust my family by making
them travel just so they could reassure themselves because I
truly felt that I had nothing that could reassure *myself*. Just the
key I had sent to Mohammed via Farida, when she found that
he had left. Thus, the key remained in my possession. Even
though I found the bus line extension to our neighborhood,
I was extremely hesitant to plunge into the adventure, so I
flagged down a petit taxi and threw myself into it after fig-
uring out where I was going. Here on the main street, where
Tensift Street branches off, there's a building where my apartment is. I stood on the street then walked toward the building
with faltering steps, like someone who would rather not get
there and not find what isn't there. I did not believe that this
was my home, but there was something of me there, something I had left there. I felt doubly out of place as I practically
threw my legs toward the building. There were some children
gathered in front playing. I didn't realize that one of them
noticed me and let the rest of them know. They all turned
to look at me. Without stopping the game, and without low-
ering their eyes from me, they kept slowly moving back and
forth where they stood. I lightened my footsteps a bit. I walked
through the front door of the building. I inserted the key with
a trembling hand. The key didn't work. I pulled it out. No! I
had put it in upside down. I tried again, the lock turned, and
the door opened. Yes, the door of my apartment opened, and
the trembling of my hand started to spread to the rest of my
body. I stepped inside. I closed the door. I found my home.
Yes! Here is the bedroom and the living room, the kitchen and
this small square space in the middle of the apartment. I felt
the desire to embrace every corner of it as if it was the first
space I had held onto after prison. I found myself in front of
myself without a shadow or a star. Dust covered everything
and spiderwebs hung from the corners, from the brown blinds

whose upper halves seemed to be a different color than the lower halves. They looked blurred. I floated between the bedroom and the living room when a hand pressing down hard on the doorbell pulled me out of this reverie. I felt my heart jump and wondered who it was. Who knew about my arrival? Maybe they were still waiting for me. That's what they had said when they delivered me to the prison administration.

There, in front of the apartment door stood practically all the women from the building. They were all gathered there and when I opened the door, they smothered me in kisses and trills. It was like getting hit on the head I was so surprised. As I welcomed them inside, I realized that the children must have told them the news. Perhaps it was the building owner who had told *them* that I had made the pilgrimage to prison. I did not know what to say. I was confused. Their warmth was palpable, and I made every effort to appear similarly warm, but I could barely mutter a few words of thanks. They stood up as I showed them to the door, still muttering words of thanks and apologizing for the empty kitchen that had nothing to drink.

When Nabil Qozah told me about how they negotiate their relationships as intellectuals or political militants with the masses there in Lebanon, and when he asked me about how we do it here, I realized that our generation eschews participation in traditional frameworks, from neighborhood to social and family occasions, and that is what creates the shock for families the moment their children are detained. Organizing the neighborhood committees, under the best of circumstances, did not go beyond accumulating militants according to where they lived. It was not based on working with people who lived in the neighborhood to solve tangible and concrete problems.

19

NIGHT FELL. I WAS COMPLETELY exhausted after having spent the entire evening cleaning the apartment. I found the gas tank empty, so I put off the bath until the following day and just washed my arms and legs. I put on my pajamas and threw myself into bed. It felt cold. I had politely declined the neighbors who invited me for lunch, and made do with some bread, olives, and cheese with tea. I made two meals of it, lunch and dinner.

I slept without knowing when or how I woke up so late the next day to the doorbell ringing. I was surprised by the smiling building owner. He greeted me warmly. I excused myself and slipped into the bedroom where I put a long robe on over my short and slightly see-through pajamas. I went back out to the landlord in the living room unsure of where to begin. The rent had accumulated yet the man had not sealed off my apartment. In fact, he was coming to me bearing greetings and congratulations for my return to freedom. What happened? Was everything nationalized while I was in there? Did the house become the property of the person who inhabits it without my knowing? He was holding a medium-sized package. I don't know how I didn't notice it before. He put it down next to the sofa. I went into the living room. I welcomed him and he greeted me again, putting his hands into his pants pocket underneath his djellaba. He pulled out an envelope. He handed it to me and, pointing to the envelope, said,

"That deposit's for you. From Mohammed."

I didn't know where Mohammed was. When I was in prison, Farida told me that he had travelled to France. I wanted to ask the building owner about him but that felt a bit awkward. How could I ask the building owner for news about Mohammed, while I didn't know a thing? And what did I want to know? The questions were bearing down on my chest, and I wasn't pretending otherwise. Quite spontaneously, he explained everything. I opened the envelope. It wasn't a letter inside. There were rent receipts. I turned them over in my hands. The rent had been paid for two years, including a rent increase of one hundred dirhams. How? I didn't know. I didn't understand a thing until he started to talk about Mohammed, about how he was "a son of the people" and how he had contacted him two years prior, as soon as I was detained.

"He's the one who told me. He was nervous and asked me to switch the rental contract from his name to yours. I would receive the rent every month. In fact, I swear to God, the man would always send it a week before the end of the month. As for the extra amount that you see there, he's the one who insisted on it. I didn't ask for a thing, but he wanted the place to remain guaranteed for you after you got out. He asked me to put the receipts in an envelope and give it to you as soon as you got here."

Where are you Mohammed and how can you break me apart whenever you please? Then you compose me and gather me right up. What I needed most right then was to bury my head in my hand and roll it around in my palm. You used to gather me together, arrange me—like documents or truths—then scatter me, and you come back now, without coming back, to gather me together yet again.

Before leaving, the old man pointed to the wrapped-up frame.

"Mohammed left this for you right before he went to France."

So, he was in France. I don't know how he settled on the idea of emigrating. He had never breathed any other air. That's how he was, or how I thought he was. I ripped the wrapping from the frame and there I was, face to face with myself. Mohammed had left me a portrait of me. He had drawn me smiling and sad. The bars were there, all around me. But behind my back. I smiled, seeing that Mohammed had dressed me in the sky-blue pajamas he loved. He would wash them when he found that I had thrown them into the basket to be washed on the weekend. He would dry them in the sun, and I'd find them laid out on the bed. I would laugh when he insisted I wear them. That's Mohammed. He connects with the small things that then become large. Just like the day he discovered four moles on my waist which filled him with joy. Over and over, he counted and measured the distance between them with his fingers. He would squeeze the flesh of my waist and the moles would draw closer to one another. Then he would relax his hand and laugh as they slid apart. From the time he discovered them until the time we split up, the four moles would remain the first things imprinted on my body by Mohammed.

Mohammed never stopped sending the rent. To this day he still sends it directly to the building owner. He is the one who made sure my housing situation was secure. I didn't know how to contact him to thank him and to ask him to stop being so generous to me. There was no possibility of returning to my job at the Arabization Institute, since I was now someone with a criminal record. I had to look for a job. The search was not difficult but it was not a comfortable choice. Some of the newspapers had begun to enrich their staff with new writers to refresh them and give them a new energy. I was among those hired at a national newspaper connected to one of the long-standing national parties. Some parties had left the government, and others had emerged to take their place. The political deck had been shuffled with some of them making it through the process. I was in no way a proponent of the newspaper's point of view because it was that of its party. Therefore, I insisted on just correcting the mistakes. Was there any job other than correcting the mistakes of those with whom the only thing you have in common is that you were both against colonialism? In fact, I only hold onto my opposition to colonialism from a history lesson I had in fifth grade. This is how power in this country becomes fixed in the seats of government, and the opposition is likewise fixed on the horizon of the uneasy question. Space here is authoritarian and it accepts the existence of the other, but without the claws or nails to injure it. It is an opposition that has to play inside its proscribed boundaries. Thus, the highest power in the country is called the opposition. They sit looking at one another and the one being sat on is told, "You need to calm things down for another three years."

And when one of those people being sat on longs for his roots, for his village back there and for his social class here of which nothing remains save for empty promises not worth the paper they're written on, it is clear that things have gotten away from him and are now in the hands of unions and mass organizations. And that's when everyone becomes indignant and wonders how this "country hick" got in here, into such a high-level meeting.

I don't know how I got to know the people living next door. More than once, Bushra and her husband, Youssef Eddahabi left their child, Mouride, at my place, especially when I brought work home from the office with me. That's how one-and-a-half-year-old Mouride came into my life, and that's how he would grow in front of me, day after day, to stand one morning on the line of years that I had carved to Gharbia, to its prison. Mouline Lyazidi is in prison. Nabil Qozah has been lost to the war. Mohammed Bassou is in France showing his paintings, standing next to a blonde woman described in the caption underneath the picture as his French wife and his artistic and emotional support. The article came for me to correct, and I was struck by Mohammed's picture in the center, headlined with his full name, showing his great relief with having his first exhibition in Paris behind him. I looked closely at Mohammed, and then at the woman, going over each letter of his name. I shrank into myself. I felt dizzy. I handed the article to my colleague, Abdelhamid Daoudi, for him to correct. I excused myself and left for home. I had started to visit Mouline, but the news moved something here inside me. How could I suffer disappointment from one love to another? Whenever longing wrote my story, separation erased it. How could I heal all the breaks in my heart from the massacre of war to the prison in the west. All I know is that one day, patience will reveal its wickedness. It will apologize to me and leave.

It wasn't the day for me to visit Mouline but I wanted to run away from memories of Mohammed to protect myself. Thus, when I run away from the west, I find myself in prison and when I escape from prison, I am embraced by the war. I was tired when I returned from visiting Mouline. I entered the apartment and took a shower. I heard a light knocking on the door, then someone pressing the doorbell. These were Mouride's knocks, I know them well. I recognize the way he rings the bell in fits and starts. He had started to grow enough so that if he stood on his tiptoes he could just barely reach the doorbell. He presses. His feet get tired. He puts them back flat on the ground then gets back up on his toes and presses the bell again. I had seen that one evening as I stood on the stairs in front of the apartment. I had come back late, and he was still insisting on seeing me before he went to sleep.

I wrapped my body in a large towel and opened the door.

"Come in Mouride! This is how you come to me, so late?! Why are you coming now? This isn't your usual morning or evening time."

"The sun visited me tonight and darkness went on and on . . . "

"And the kids who fill the world with song, where'd they go?"

"They were riding here," and he pointed to a plastic truck he still dragged around. "They invite the streets to a joyous banquet of trilling and go off to their evenings."

"Come on in, Mouride."

He stepped inside. He was a little man the height of a child. He takes off his plastic sandals to jump into my bed like the cat I thought I heard meowing one day. I am on the edge of wakefulness, hanging in a room prepared for what comes before the investigation, dried drops of blood. The first thing that welcomes me as I emerge from unconsciousness. He says,

"I came for you to tell me a story."

I thought hard about choosing an appropriate story that would be outside of the known repertoire. Without Hdidan's face peering from it, or a ghoul's head looking out from an unknown cavern or from a naked past.

Mouride noticed me wavering for a bit too long, so he chimed in saying,

"I want one of those stories about today and tomorrow, not about yesterday."

"Do you mean a story of the past, where things began, or a story of the present and future that's covered in dust and rises up at the end? All the candles you see in the room are for tonight, but you won't find anyone to light them."

Just like my body.

"And you?"

Me?

Where am I going to win the love of the coming days? In wanting dead soil in my eye or by the promises of every likely winter? Just tell me how I can erase this fear. By looking at the sun? Or through an assault I didn't commit? Listen, Mouride! You're too old to just listen. I'll present a character, and you fill in the details.

He agreed that we work together to come up with an improvised bedtime story. He asked who the hero was, and I told him that he looks like him. Not an angel, but he's purer than humans. Then Mouride cut me off. "Then he doesn't lie." So, I added, "Because he's bold." And he cut me off. "He isn't afraid." He asked for some water. I handed him the glass while looking into his eyes and reading in them everything that bars cannot hold back, wishing I could tell him: "If only you knew that angels were, at every decisive moment, shackled in chains that were fastened by friends." Mouride brought me out of my reveries, asking about the hero's enemies and who they were. I thought. What names would I give him? The night guards? The Commander? The passing flare-up of violence in a crowd? A car that doesn't stop for a red light? So, I suggested he finish drinking his water first and then we'd finish the story together . . .